CHILDREN OF THE
REALM

Lauren Stabler

Edited and proofread by Rebecca Holmes Editing

Cover and design by Miblart

Second Edition, 2023

IBSN-13: 979-8352507421

To all the girls just trying to survive in this world.

CHAPTER ONE

I sit on the damp sand, trailing patterns with my fingers. My hair is being whipped around my face by the warm September wind, I've given up the battle to keep it back. We go home today, me and Isaac.

Home.

The sea roars in the distance, dragging away a line of white lace as the tide lowers for the first time today and crashes against a forgotten ship, held fast by an anchor. Beaches are still open to the public, but the wealthy don't care for boat rides and the poor can no longer afford them.

They were taken away when our joy was.

The sense of peace I once felt when by the sea no longer fills me. Instead, I feel only longing. For a time when these sands were filled with children's laughter, for a time it felt like I could call a place like this my *true* home, the home of my heart. I don't know where that is anymore.

I'd always wanted to live by the sea. Told my parents that I would do exactly that "when I'm rich". I'm not poor anymore. I don't know what I am. I have money, but it's not mine. It comes with conditions. I'm always watched, always escorted somewhere. If I look over my right shoulder now, at the road above the beach, I'll be able to see the security detail assigned to protect us. To watch us. I get the feeling they're waiting for us to mess up somehow. And I can't just use that money to move here. I have to live where they tell me to.

With a sigh, Isaac sits down behind me, bringing his legs to either side of my body. I lean back against him and let him wrap his arms around my waist. He kisses the top of my head.

'Are you ready?' he asks.

I can feel my shoulders tense. There are so many things coming that we need to be ready for. So much I can't prepare myself for.

'For what?' I ask.

'To go home. Start university. I don't know.'

I shrug. Going back means seeing Charmaine. Things haven't been the same since that day in the woods.

'Addy, we want you to join us,' she said.

I stared at her, she sat with her jaw tight and back straight. She clenched and unclenched her fists multiple times. I couldn't tell if she really wanted me to accept her offer, but she was determined to get the yes.

'Why now?' I asked.

'We could use someone like you on the inside.'

'Use.'

She sighed. 'You know what I mean.'

I stood up and crossed my arms. 'I'm not sure I do. And I'm not sure I want to.'

'Addy...' She approached me, a pained look crossing her face and I sighed.

'I don't know,' I answered truthfully. Yes, I wanted to get back at the government for the trials, but I didn't know whether this was the right way, or if I was even the right person. The uncertainty of what they wanted me to do didn't help either.

She nodded. 'I understand. We'll give you some time. But we can't wait forever.'

But that was six months ago, and I still haven't given her an answer. She'll be expecting one today, I think, when we get back to London. With everything happening tomorrow.

I run a hand through my hair and look up at Isaac, kissing his jaw. He's let stubble grow while we've had all this time to do nothing, but I bet he'll shave it before we start university tomorrow.

While things have been quiet with Charmaine, things have been great with Isaac. We've been able to date in a way we wouldn't have been able to if I was still at the orphanage. London is the city with the highest population in The Realm of Great Britain. The restaurants are still open, and even though we can afford to pay, we always receive free service because everyone knows who we are after the trials. It sends a pang of guilt through me each time, so I leave a fifty percent tip. They need the money more than I do.

We're taking our relationship slowly, too. Everything happened so rapidly during the trials, we didn't want it to feel rushed anymore. We needed to make sure this was real before we jumped into anything serious. Of course, that hasn't been without its obstacles. We barely

3

got through the first interview after the trials. A catch up with all the winners to see how we were faring. They pushed Isaac and I together for the interviews, trying to ask how our relationship was. But it wasn't anything yet. We were both still processing everything that had just happened, everything we had seen. We didn't have the mental space. The interview was hard, and I could barely speak, but at least I didn't have to see Janesh. I haven't forgiven him for his part in all the death.

We decided we needed to get away this weekend, just the two of us, before all the crazy comes back into our life. We're officially a couple now, and I couldn't be happier about the decision. I've never needed anyone like I need Isaac. Every part of my body aches for him.

He looks down at me, his skin flushes and he flicks his tongue out, wetting his lips. I can't help but watch his every movement.

A smile tugs at the corner of his mouth. 'Why don't you stay over tonight?'

A breath hitches in my throat. We haven't spent the night together since the trials, and as much as I want it, I don't know if I'm ready for him to see what happens at night.

He must see the hesitation on my face, and he strokes a thumb along my jaw, tipping it up to meet his lips in a long, soft kiss before pulling away. 'If you're not ready—'

'That's not it,' I say quickly. I'm more than ready for *that*. I chew my lip, indecision gnawing at me. I'm scared to tell him, I realise. Scared he'll think I'm not the person he's been getting to know for months. Scared of not being strong. My stomach turns to lead. He saw me at my lowest during the trials. This is nothing compared to that, so I tell him. 'It's the nightmares.'

His eyes darken and he clenches his jaw. 'Yeah, I get them too.'

I look back towards what's left of the sea. 'I wake myself up so much, either crying or screaming, and I don't want you to have to deal with that.'

I can feel his chest hitch against my back, and he slides away, kneeling in front of me so we're facing each other. 'Stop that.' His eyes bore into me. 'I want you—no, I *need* you to know that it's not something I have to *deal with.* I want to be there for you in every way, if you'll let me.'

My eyes dampen. I don't know why I thought this would be the thing to make him cower away from me. What's one more time crying into his shoulder, when we have a lifetime in front of us?

I nod and give him a small smile. 'Then yes, I'll stay tonight.' I grimace, knowing what waits for me at home. 'But I need to see Charmaine first.'

He sighs. 'Is she going to be pissed that you missed her birthday?'

I shake my head. 'We had a mini celebration before we came here. It's fine.'

When Charmaine wasn't reminding me about the Children of the Realm, it was almost like we could be real friends again. Like there was nothing stopping us from catching up on the time lost in the orphanage. Watching movies that hadn't been banned, drinking wine, and talking about our lives from *before*. But the night always ends, it always comes back to the same conversation. And I never have an answer.

'Come on,' Isaac says, standing and trying to wipe the sand off his jeans. The sand is still damp though, and just sticks to his skin. He holds his hand out for me and helps me stand. The sand grinds against my skin. 'Back to reality.'

5

He starts walking to the car, but I turn to look back at the sea and around us at the quiet seaside town, as a lump forms in my throat.

The quiet can't last forever.

CHAPTER TWO

We barely speak on our trip back to London, lost in our own thoughts. As the tall buildings start climbing around us, a heaviness sets upon me. I never felt claustrophobic in cities until I won the trials and moved here. Now, it's like the towers close in on me, and I know it's only going to get worse from tomorrow.

Too soon, we pull up to our block of flats and get out of the car. We ride the lift together and stop outside my front door. Isaac's is only across the hall. My mind flashes back to the first time we came here and stood in this exact way, facing each other with a goodbye on our lips like it was the end of something.

Isaac grasps my hand, rubbing his thumb across the back of it, his eyes sparkling with anticipation. He leans down to kiss me, but we're interrupted by my front door opening.

I turn to greet Charmaine, but my throat closes, and I can't speak.

James saunters out.

His dark brown hair glistens with water, like he just got out of the shower. I grit my teeth. I told Charmaine I didn't want him in the flat. We can't trust him. Not after our relationship years ago, when he left me to grieve his death. What's one more lie to him?

I straighten and mask my face with boredom. I won't give him the pleasure of seeing me shocked by his presence. As if he still has any effect on me.

'What are you doing here, James?' I ask, one arm crossed over my chest, as I pick my nails with my other hand.

He smirks. 'I wanted to see you, but obviously you weren't here, so I hung out with Charmaine for a bit.'

I raise my eyebrows. Questions about what they would even do together spring to my mind, but I push them away and try to dismiss him. 'Time to go then.'

He leans against the doorframe and crosses his arms. 'Aw, don't be like that, honeybun.'

'Don't call me that. You lost that right when you faked your death.' I glare at him and fold my arms.

Behind me, Isaac coughs, and I relax my shoulders slightly. I was so caught up in my anger, I almost forgot he was here.

James pushes around me. 'You must be Isaac.' He holds his hand out, demanding a handshake.

Isaac narrows his eyes at him but shakes his hand firmly. 'Yeah. And you are?'

'Didn't Adelaide tell you?' He drops his hand and cocks his head. 'I'm James, the ex-boyfriend.'

Isaac furrows his brows. 'Aren't you supposed to be dead?'

James chuckles. 'I'm sure that would make things easier, wouldn't it, Addy?'

I roll my eyes but don't acknowledge the comment, turning to Isaac. 'Yeah, he's supposed to be dead, but he *miraculously* came back to life in February.'

'I see,' Isaac says with a straight face, and I sigh. This better not mess up our night. 'I'll let you two talk then, I guess, see you later?'

He leans down and brushes his lips against mine and I smile at his trust. Picking up his bag, he turns, and lets himself into his flat.

I turn back to James, who raises an eyebrow at me. 'Are you leaving then or what?'

He smirks again. 'Yeah, before I go though, have you given any more thought to our proposition?'

I sigh. Yes. I've been overthinking it for months, but I don't want him to know that, so I shrug. 'Maybe, maybe not. Either way, I don't have an answer for you. Not one you'd like anyway.'

'Tick tock, honeybun.' I bristle but don't say anything. I'm sure rejecting the name again would just satisfy him and I don't want that. 'We need you. Remember that.' He leans towards me and grabs a strand of my hair as if to brush it back, but I jerk away from him. 'I still love your hair, you know.'

'I don't really care, James.' I elbow past him into my flat, slamming the door behind me.

I look around the flat but see no sign of Charmaine. Since moving in six months ago, we've redecorated. It's still open plan, but the walls of the living room and dining room are now a jade green, and we've added black and gold everywhere. The sofa matches the wall with black cushions and a swirling gold design. We kept the kitchen the same, the breakfast counter and sides are a marbled white with grey cupboards below and hanging over. We exchanged the plain white plates for a set of grey ones with branches stencilled on. The hidden built-in fridge means we can't stick magnets on, but we blu-tacked some photos to it instead. In the last six months, we've managed to explore all of London together. We tried to take lots of photos of ourselves actually having fun, like if we didn't capture the moment, we might not believe it was ever real. There are a few of me and Isaac on there as well.

'Charmaine?' I shout, just as a shower starts running. I roll my eyes at her obvious way of avoiding me. 'Whatever, I didn't want to talk to you anyway,' I mutter.

I go to my room and dump my bag on the fluffy black rug at the end of my bed. The only things I kept in this room were the TV and mattress. I painted the walls in wisteria purple, giving me a small sense of wistfulness. After winning the trials, I'd asked if I could have something of Celeste's, but they refused. So, I kept her favourite colour for myself, and now I'm surrounded by her in my safe space. My nightmares chase me awake so often that I've become attuned to the night now, and I've decorated my room with twinkling fairy lights and moon motifs.

I lay back on my mattress, letting it mould to my body again. I was only away for three nights but the air in here feels stale, like I don't really live here and could be gone at any second. Which I guess is true. When we moved in, we checked every room for hidden cameras. They're almost invisible, but when you look closely, you can see tiny lenses in the corners of almost all the rooms. One slip up, and this could all be taken from me.

I undress, unbothered about the people behind the cameras seeing me naked after everything they put me through in the trials. What's one more humiliation? I go into my own en-suite bathroom, turning on the shower. I stand under the waterfall and let it wash away the scent of travelling. I have big plans for my night with Isaac and I need to be at my best. I shave everything, and lather myself in vanilla and honey body wash, breathing in the scent and letting my mind wander to tonight. I don't know what I'm going to wear, but with my monthly stipend, I've been able to afford nicer underwear than ever before, and anything will be better than the knickers I was wearing during the trials, when Isaac and I touched properly for the first time. The night before I lost Celeste. Her lifeless face fills my vision, her eyes open and empty as I repeatedly scream for her to wake up. Tears fall from my eyes and the walls inside me crumble. I'm there again, back in the trials. I might as well have never left.

I take in a sharp breath and cast the memory away. They haunt my nightmares enough; I don't need to see them during my waking hours too. Although I need the pain to remind myself I'm not the same person I was when I started the trials. I'll take it wherever I go. *My name is Adelaide Taylor, and I will not let them break me.*

I tell myself the same thing daily. It almost works, almost removes the fear.

I step out of the shower, patting myself dry, before returning to my room and putting on a pair of lacy black knickers and a matching bra. I pull on a short black dress, and I'm almost ready.

The click of the door to the room next to mine signals that Charmaine is out of the shower, and I rush out of the room without brushing my hair.

11

'Charmaine!'

She jumps at the sound of my voice and turns around, looking at me sheepishly.

'I know what you're going to say,' she says.

'Well, tell me then,' I say, cocking an eyebrow and crossing my arms.

She sighs. 'I know you don't want James here, but we were just watching TV, I swear. We weren't discussing... that thing.' She looks around at the cameras in the corners of the room. One mention of her rebel faction and we'd be thrown in prison. Probably back into the trials, what with it being for criminals now. The thought makes me internally shudder.

'He looked like he'd had a shower.' I run a hand through the tangles of my wet hair and sigh. 'Look, if there's something going on between you two, you can just tell me. Me and James are over. Done. Completely.'

She rolls her eyes. 'Did you forget I'm gay?'

I shrug. 'No, but—I don't know. Things change.'

She just looks at me. 'Believe me, I will never like guys.'

I laugh. I don't know why she'd suddenly change sexuality just because I'm paranoid about him being around. 'Yeah. I know. I'm being stupid.'

'Yes, you are.' She smiles and pulls me into a hug, and we collapse onto the sofa. 'How was your holiday?'

I lean my head back, looking at the white ceiling. 'It was good, relaxing. Just what I needed before tomorrow.'

'Did you and Isaac finally fuck?'

I sit up straight and push her jokingly. 'Charmaine!' I exclaim with a laugh.

She chuckles back. 'What, can't a friend be curious?'

'Yes, but you don't need to be so crass.' I go back to staring at the ceiling.

Charmaine lays her head next to mine. 'That doesn't answer my question.'

'No. Tonight is the night, I think.'

'Finally!' She beams at me, and I grin back, getting up from the sofa. 'Right, your hair. We need to sort it out.'

'What do you mean?' I pluck at the ends.

'Have you even brushed it?' She stands and lifts one of my tangles with a grimace.

'Well, no, but I came out here to talk to you first.'

'Enough of that, back to your room. Let's get you ready.'

We spend the next hour gossiping about our exes and the non-existent sex life we've had since we were forced to live at the orphanage. The Madame would have punished us severely if she'd ever found someone else in our beds. Not that we would have done it there anyway when we were sharing rooms with multiple other women. Aside from that, we never had time between work and our chores at the orphanage to even think about it. At least, I didn't. Charmaine could have but she was too busy with Children of the Realm.

She dries and curls my hair loosely. I chew the inside of my mouth, suddenly jittery about the night ahead of me. I shouldn't be nervous. I've done this before. Many times. Well, maybe not many, but enough times to know what I'm doing. Maybe it's because it's with someone I actually care about. Someone I could love, given the chance.

Charmaine gives me a wink when I'm ready. I stand in front of my full-length mirror. The dress hugs all the curves I've gained since I left the trials, and I can't help but feel sexy for the first time in a long time. I hope Isaac feels the same way.

I forgo putting shoes on, only needing to cross the hall to Isaac's flat.

I knock timidly on the door, my stomach doing somersaults. I feel sick and I'm sweating. *Jesus, Adelaide, get a grip of yourself.* But what if he isn't ready to be woken up by me crying or screaming? What if that scares him away? No. It won't. I shake myself. He's already seen that part of me—during the trials. It'll be fine. Why am I thinking about the trials again? The one thing I want to forget the most. I groan just as Isaac opens the door.

His eyes run up and down my body hungrily, and with a grin, he pulls me into the flat and shuts the door.

CHAPTER THREE

The silence is interrupted only by the buzz of energy kindling between Isaac and me. He stares at me, like we haven't seen each other for a long time, and I can feel his gaze touch me everywhere. I bite my lip and my mouth moistens. He keeps hold of my hand. Nothing is said as we stand here, taking each other in, waiting for what is to come.

'Hi,' he finally says a little breathlessly, one side of his mouth twitching up.

I step forward and press a kiss to his lips, slowly, letting my body melt against his. He's kept in shape since the trials, and I can feel every inch of the hardness of his body as he brings his arms around me, drawing me ever closer.

His fingers trail down my spine as I deepen our kiss. A shudder goes through me as he pushes me against the door, letting me know just how much he wants this. I run my hands through his hair, down his neck, and across his chest.

He pulls away for a moment. 'Are you real?'

I smirk. 'I think so. But if you need to touch more of me to find out, go right ahead.'

I pull his head back to me, opening my mouth, and letting his tongue meet mine in a battle. His hands trace the length of my back, coming round to the front of my body. His right lands on my breast and he sucks in a breath. I smile against his mouth and urge him on. His left hand traces a path along my hip before cupping my ass. I can feel my heartbeat deep down in my core. My hands shake as I hold back, letting him explore further. I've wanted this for so long, pined for it even. I feel like each touch could make me explode. His hand dips further, finding the bottom of my dress, moving underneath so he can feel my skin. I begin unbuttoning his shirt slowly, revealing his chest beneath my hands inch by inch. Once he is exposed to me, I push it off his shoulders. He removes his hands for a moment, to take it off the rest of the way. He pulls his mouth away from mine, pleasure sparkling in his eyes. He drops before me, lifting the bottom of my dress, standing to push it further up my body. I lift my arms so he can take it off completely. I stand before him, in nothing but my underwear. He stands back, his eyes memorising every inch of me, turning me into a puddle beneath his stare.

His lips meet mine with a renewed ferocity. His hands grip the backs of my legs, urging me up. He lifts me, so my centre is pressed against him, and I can feel every hard inch of him through his jeans. I relish the feel of him, inch by remarkable inch. I gulp in anticipation, and he smiles against my lips.

He pulls me away from the door and carries me across the room to his bedroom. He kicks the door shut behind him, before laying me back on his bed. I sit up and raise my eyebrows at him.

'Why are your jeans still on?' I ask.

He pulls them off, so he's stood before me in his boxers. I look him up and down, appreciating the work he's done in the gym downstairs. He's gained muscled, but not so much that they look strained. His abs tense and I'm sure he could throw me on the bed with ease if I wanted him to. The thought makes me tingle.

He moves towards the bed, but I put a hand up, stopping him with a small smile. I lift my hand behind my back slowly, unhooking my bra and slipping it off, throwing it on the floor. A hungry look takes over his face, making my nipples peak. He draws his bottom lip between his teeth. *Fuck.* I let him lay over me. He kisses me briefly, then trails his lips along my jaw, my neck, my chest. He takes my right nipple between his teeth, teasing slightly, as he circles my other one with his fingers. I come loose, leaning my head back against his soft headboard.

'Fuck me,' I breathe.

He chuckles against my breast; the vibrations send a shiver through me. He moves down my body and hooks my knickers from my hips with his thumbs. I can't take it; I just need him to touch me again. His fingers trail the inside of my thighs, making me squirm. Finally, he draws a finger along my centre, finding out just how ready I am for him.

He raises his eyebrows at me. 'So wet already. I wanted to take my time with you,' he says.

'I've waited too long,' I say, cocking my head to one side. 'This time.'

'I completely agree,' he says, almost growling.

He removes his boxers and lays himself back over me.

He stops, his face so close to most to mine, and pulls back. 'I just want to check, do I need to use a condom?' he asks.

I smile. 'We both got tested recently, didn't we?' He nods, this was a conversation we had a few months ago before we were both ready. We're both clear of everything. 'I'm on the best pill there is now as well. As far as I'm aware, there's only a ninety-nine-percent chance of it failing. And I track all of that on an app. We're good. Is that okay?'

He grins. 'That sounds great to me,' he says.

I pull him down for a slow kiss as he lines himself up with me. Slowly, so slowly, he pushes himself inside. A moan escapes me as I get what I've been craving. He pushes himself up onto his forearms as he lets himself settle inside me. My hand meets his face.

'You're perfect,' I say, kissing him again.

He pulls out of me quickly, drawing back again, making me moan against his lips. I feel him smile.

He moves in me, against me. My hands move around to his back, gripping him to me, my nails digging into his skin, as I press my breasts against his chest.

He groans. And hooks a hand behind my knee, drawing it up to his hip, so he can move deeper inside.

We go slowly, wanting to savour each other.

When we both find our release, I exhale against his shoulder heavily.

'Again,' I breathe.

'Give me a second,' he says, kissing my neck.

Without warning, he slams back into me, making me moan his name.

'Say that again,' he says.

He pulls out and once again, claims me with a thrust. I give into his demand and give my entire self to him, exploding with each new thrust. I could do this forever.

We lie facing each other, every inch of our bodies coated in glimmering sweat. I crave more, but I want to take my time getting to know this part of him. He smiles and pushes my hair behind my ear.

'You hungry?' he asks.

My stomach growls in anger, making me laugh. 'Apparently.'

He gets out of bed, letting me see all of him, electrifying my core. He puts his boxers on and leans down to give me a kiss.

'I'll make some food. Anything you fancy?'

I bite my lip, thinking. 'Okay, don't judge me for this. But I really want Yorkshire puddings and pizza.'

He looks at me like I just said I want to murder a puppy. 'Together?'

'Yeah, it's not that weird, I promise.'

'I must really like you,' he says with a laugh. 'Yorkshire puddings and pizza it is.'

I grin at his back as he leaves the room. This night has been perfect. It's the first time I've forgotten the trials, and all the pain that came with them.

With a sigh, I get out of bed and hunt around for my knickers. They must be here somewhere. Oh, on the windowsill. I put them on, and then the shirt Isaac was wearing. I breathe in his smell—cinnamon and pine—and let it overwhelm me for a moment. I'd be happy to spend forever in this room, escape the world, the government, what's to come. But reality will hit me soon enough. I need to enjoy this small pocket of time away from the world.

I go into Isaac's kitchen, almost identical to my own, and wrap my arms around his naked waist and rest my chin on his shoulder. He's stirring the Yorkshire pudding mix, and my god, if that's not the sexiest thing I've ever seen. I trail a finger up and down the centre of his abs, and he leans back against me.

'If you keep doing that we'll never get to eat.'

I back away.

I lean against the breakfast counter, and he turns towards me, with the jug in his hand, thick batter dripping from the whisk.

'We should talk,' he says finally.

My stomach clenches. Does he regret this, what we just did?

He takes a tray out of the oven and carefully sets it on the side. He pours the mixture into each slot. Some of it spills over the side, but I won't complain. I've always loved the extra bits that came with the puddings. Once finished, he places it back into the heat before turning to me.

He puts one arm either side of me on the counter. 'Don't look so worried.'

'Do you regret it?' I ask quickly, not meeting his eyes in case I see the truth in them.

'Regret what?' he asks with a frown.

'Us, what we just did.'

'God, no, Addy.' He wipes his face with his hand. 'I could never regret any moment with you. I lo—really like you. You know that, right?'

What was he about to say before he corrected himself?

My shoulders sag in relief and I grin up at him. 'I really like you too.' I take a breath. 'What do we need to talk about?'

'James.'

I freeze. I knew this was coming, I just didn't think it would be today. But after the awkward moment in the hallway, I guess it was to be expected.

I sigh and he backs away, leaning against the counter opposite me with his arms crossed.

'There is no James,' I say, and it's true. He's nothing to me anymore.

'Then what was earlier about?' I don't answer and he continues, 'Look, I won't be one of those couples that doesn't communicate. We've been through too much together to lie to each other, okay?'

I nod. He's right. I don't know why answering him honestly is making my throat constrict so much. I look up at where I assume the cameras in the flat are, and back at Isaac.

'I can't tell you everything right now.'

'But—'

'I want to, really, I do. But, you know.' I look at the cameras from the corner of my eye again and his face relaxes, he gets it. I don't know if they listen to our conversations, but hopefully that wasn't too suspicious if they do.

'Okay, we can talk about that another time, that's fine. But why is he here?'

I shrug. 'Him and Charmaine are friends apparently.'

'And he's just been hanging around your flat?'

I shake my head. 'Not while I've been there, no. As far as I know, this was the first time he was there. I don't want him there. I don't trust him.'

He nods. 'That's fair. I just need to know something.' He takes a deep breath and runs a hand through his hair before looking me straight in the eye. 'Do you still have feelings for him?'

I stiffen. Do I? When I see him, I still feel something, but it doesn't feel like love. It doesn't even feel like what we had when we were together, whatever that was. It doesn't feel like what I have with Isaac. I know my answer. 'No. He'll always have a piece of me, but the piece of me he has isn't the person I am anymore. I'm okay with that. But I don't want him in my life. There's only you.'

His shoulders relax and he comes over to me again, wrapping his arms around my waist and drawing me in for a kiss.

'That's all I needed to hear,' he says against my lips, and I smile.

I could get used to this.

Chapter Four

A sharp wail pierces the air and my eyes snap open to darkness. Where am I? My breath hitches in my throat as I sit up, letting my dream come back to me. I was outside a tent in the dark woods and a wet growl cleaved through the air. I couldn't see anyone as I begged to be let into one of the tents, any of them. But each tent stayed quiet. And then I swore I could feel warm breath on the back of my neck and goosebumps rose on my arms.

But as I turned to see it, I woke myself up with a scream.

All I can hear now is the buzz in my head as I try to figure out where I am. I'm covered in an unfamiliar quilt. The smell invades my senses, cinnamon and pine. I close my eyes and let it overtake me, pushing away the buzzing in my head, and letting myself hear and feel everything else.

Someone is stroking my hair and telling me everything is okay. Isaac.

A light turns on behind me and casts my shadow across the wall at the end of the bed. I breathe a sigh of relief. I can't stand the dark anymore.

'I'm sorry,' Isaac says, and I turn to him.

'What for?'

'I should have left a light on.'

'You couldn't have known. Heck, I've been sleeping with a light on for so long now, it's just become second nature to me.'

'What was your nightmare about?'

I wince. I've never voiced the nightmares before, not even to Charmaine. 'I-I,' I stutter. I close my eyes and take a deep breath, trying to stop myself shaking. Isaac doesn't speak, waiting for me to calm myself so I can tell him. I open my eyes. 'I was back in the first trial. That first night. But I wasn't in the tent, I was outside trying to get in. Waiting to be caught by whatever was out there.' I run a hand down my face, and I tremble. 'God, the fear. I really felt like I was there. I can't even imagine what Brett must have felt in that moment.'

Isaac pulls me back, laying my head against his chest so he can stroke my hair. 'I've had that dream once or twice. I think it's the not knowing. But most of all, it's the guilt.' I nod against his chest. 'But it wasn't our fault. You know that, right? We'd be dead, too, if we'd done anything.'

I nod again. I try to tell myself that constantly. We couldn't have fought whatever it was that killed Brett. We'll never know what it was, though. Sometimes, I think that's worse.

The terror left over from the dream starts to dissipate and my chest lightens.

'My name is Adelaide Taylor, and I will not let them break me,' I whisper.

Isaac pulls me tighter against his chest. 'I tell myself the same thing.'

I look at the clock on the bedside table, and it's already six a.m. If I don't get up now, I won't be able to go for a run before we get picked up for university.

'I need to go,' I say, getting out of bed.

Isaac frowns. 'So early?'

'Yeah, I don't know what time we'll be back, so I want to get my run done now.' I lean down and give him a quick kiss. It sends a spark through my entire body, and I could easily stay in bed. But if the trials have taught me anything, it's that I never want to be out of shape again. I don't know what's coming. 'I'll see you outside at eight?'

'Sure. I'm gonna sleep some more.'

I roll my eyes. 'Jealous.'

He smirks at me, and I pick my clothes off the floor and make my way back to my own flat.

A sleek black car with tinted windows pulls up outside our building at exactly eight, and Isaac and I get into the back. Every time we're taken somewhere, there's always a new car smell. I don't know if they put the smell in, or if they're actually new.

I was right, Isaac has shaved for today. His face is smoother than I've ever seen it. I can't help missing the stubble.

He looks over at me and cocks an eyebrow. 'What's wrong?'

'I'm not sure about this look,' I say, touching his jaw.

'Oh? And what do you prefer?' His lips twitch up.

I don't want the driver knowing all our business, so I lean in to whisper, 'I like the tickle of your beard, if I'm being honest.'

He clears his throat. 'Tickle where?'

I smile and sit back. He grabs my hand and squeezes three times.

I needed the momentary distraction. My stomach feels like it could empty at any second, but there isn't anything in there. I've been to university before, I don't know why I'm so anxious about it. Maybe because they haven't let us pick our courses yet. I'd still love to continue my veterinary studies, but at this point, the course is probably already full. There are so many unknowns before us.

The last six months have been a great way to try to move past the anxiety of the unknown, but this feels the same as when we first arrived at the trial centre. And I don't want to know what that means. My gut tells me it isn't good, but I'm trying to ignore it.

I chew the inside of my cheek as I watch London disappear. We'll be studying at the University of London, which is now top in the country above Cambridge and Oxford, but we don't know which campus we're going to. I've never travelled through this area.

I lean forwards so the driver can hear me. 'Excuse me.' He turns his head slightly to acknowledge me, and I continue, 'How long until we get to where we're going?'

'Should be about forty-five minutes, miss. We're going out to Egham in Surrey.'

'Why is it part of the University of London if it's in Surrey?' I ask with a frown.

He laughs. 'Beats me, love. I think it's one of the old campuses, and they love their old buildings, don't they?'

We both know who *they* are without having to say it. All the old buildings, campuses, schools, and town halls have been turned into something useful for the government. The first stages of the trials were even in an old boarding school. It gives them a sense of class, I guess. They want to look good, traditional. Well, they're definitely not progressive, that's for sure. I lean back in my seat and stare out of the window.

I feel disconnected from my body as the car stops. I focus on the building we've pulled in front of. Red brick everywhere. Someone opens my door for me, and I unbuckle my seatbelt and get out of the car. The air is quiet. Nobody else is around ready to start their first day. That's weird. Maybe it isn't the real first day for everyone, and we need a different induction so we can choose our courses?

Grass stretches in front of the tall building. Are those actual turrets in the corners? How old even is this building? It could be a castle if it didn't feel so suffocating.

Isaac steps besides me and links his fingers with mine, taking it all in with me. This is where we'll be studying for the next three years. I could never have dreamed to afford this, or to live here, even before student loans were scrapped. It's almost imposing enough to make me want to go back to the flat, but I don't. I straighten my back and squeeze Isaac's hand once before letting go. I can do this. I won't be afraid.

The woman who let me out of the car clears her throat. 'Follow me, please.'

She leads us up a wide set of stone steps into the building. The building is a square shape, with halls surrounding a quad area we're told is for staff only, so we go the long way around to the opposite end.

We pass few people on the way. I would have thought today would be everyone's induction day, or at least move in day, but maybe it's too early right now.

We finally stop outside an office with the name "Helen Hale" written on a plaque attached to a mahogany door. The woman opens it for us, and we enter, before she shuts it behind us, and her footsteps disappear. The room is large, with five bookcases at least four foot wide and high enough to need a ladder lining one wall. I don't bother trying to look at the names of the books, I doubt me and Helen have the same tastes. We haven't spoken to her since the day we left the trials and she tried to convince me everything we'd just been through was all out of the generosity of the government. I didn't want to push her and lose everything just as I'd received it. I thought we were done with her then.

A granddaughter clock sits in the corner, ticking. An executive pedestal desk sits in the middle of the room—I only know the name because I thought about getting one for our flat—it's dark oak and aged, suggesting it was here long before Helen was even born. From what I remember, she's in her late forties. A high-backed leather chair is tucked in behind it. In front of the desk are four, green velvet armchairs that match the top of the desk. The two on either end are already occupied.

Janesh sits to the right, eyeing us curiously. Indignation rises inside me, as I think of all the deaths he caused during the trials, and I push my nails into the palms of my hands, trying not to let the past dictate me. On the left sits a woman with long, platinum blonde hair French plaited down her back. She turns and I realise she's Ivy. She looks different with her hair dyed but it works well with the darkness of her skin. Her back is straight, and she has a smile on her face. Considering

Janesh killed her girlfriend, Violet, during the trials, I would have thought she'd be simmering. But I can't see any animosity on her face.

I'll never forget the arrow protruding from Violet's eye. I don't know how Ivy can sit in the same room as Janesh without reacting.

Isaac takes the seat next to Janesh, knowing without my saying that I need space from him. He tried to sabotage both of us at some point during the trials, neither of us want to be around him but I appreciate the small gesture.

I take the seat next to Ivy and smile at her.

'How are you doing?' I ask.

'I'm good,' she says overenthusiastically, and frowns slightly like she didn't mean it to come out that way. She clears her throat and continues, 'I just moved to London last week. Helen decided she wanted me closer to the university than Liverpool, so my family and I have been given a penthouse in Knightsbridge.'

My eyebrows shoot up. I thought my flat was ridiculous, but a penthouse must cost a fortune.

'Jesus, that's amazing. How do you think the government afforded that?'

She looks around like she doesn't want anyone else to hear but it doesn't matter, nobody walks past our room. It's like we have the entire building to ourselves but that can't be true. Her eyes dart to Janesh and narrow slightly. She's not as happy as she seems, then. She looks back at me and says with a low voice, 'As far as I know, the family that lived there before were part of a rebellion, so the government took ownership of the property. Now we get to reap the rewards.'

I frown slightly at the cavalier way she says that. It's highly likely the family was executed for their involvement in a rebellion, but she doesn't seem to care. I do wonder what they had to rebel against, the system was made for them.

Before I can respond, Janesh interrupts us. 'Adelaide?'

I whip around to him, shocked that he'd try to speak to me. I don't answer.

He clears his throat. 'I just wanted to say to you—to all of you, really—I'm really sorry for everything that happened in the trials. I didn't have a choice; you've got to under—'

Helen walks into the room before he can finish, and he falls silent. He looks down at his hands.

Why do I have to understand what he did? I could have been killed in the maze. Celeste *was* killed during the escape room, that wasn't his fault, but he didn't seem to care. He's got no excuse for Heather, though. Or Violet, especially. He owes Ivy more than an apology, but I don't think his words will ever be enough.

Helen sits behind her desk and smiles widely at us all. 'Welcome to Royal Holloway, you will be completing your studies here for the next three years.'

'Erm,' I say, raising my hand like I'm in school. 'Helen?'

'It's Miss Hale now you'll be studying here. I am the head of your course. Although I won't be teaching you directly most of the time.'

I frown slightly at that; I didn't know she was a tutor. 'Okay, Miss Hale. When can we pick what courses we'll be studying?'

The other three lean forward eagerly. It looks like Ivy and Janesh haven't been given the chance to pick either.

'Ah, about that,' she says, picking up four folders and handing them out to each of us. Our names are written on the front and inside are multiple sheets of paper. I don't take them out to read though, and instead, wait for what she has to tell us. 'After how well you all did in the trials, we've decided you'll be great additions to the politics course this year.'

'What?' Isaac says. 'But I don't have any interest—' Helen raises a hand to stop him.

'You *will* let me finish.' She glares at Isaac, and he leans back in his seat. I give him a sympathetic look, agreeing with him, but unable to voice my concerns. 'Now, you all did so well with how you solved all the puzzles and worked together. The way some of you took leadership is exactly what we look for in our government. I understand this may not be something you initially thought you were interested in, but once you start, you'll see how perfect you all are for it.'

Isaac leans his elbows on his knees. 'And if we say no?' he asks.

She raises an eyebrow. 'I don't see any reason why you would say no, but if you choose not to take the course, you will lose your place at the university.' That's it? I'd rather leave university than be forced to do the course. By the look on her face, she knows this is what we all think. She smirks and continues, 'Not only will you lose your place at university, but your stipend will also be stopped, and we will evict you from your properties. Now, any questions?'

CHaPTer FIVe

The ticking of the clock behind the desk is the only sound in the room. What could any of us say? If we decide to give everything up now, there'd be nowhere for us to go. I won't go back to an orphanage, but I've got another eight months until I'm legally allowed to live alone. Isaac is twenty-five in January, but until then, we'd have to live with supervision. And even then, I could only live with him if we got married.

I'm getting ahead of myself. Politics will be fine, I'm sure. I bet I can make a good career out of that. And politicians still make good money. I'll never want for anything again.

But if it's so easy for them to take everything from us now, could they pull the rug out from under us in the future? My chest tightens and my breath quickens as my new reality closes in. It was fun playing freedom while it lasted, but we might as well be back in the trials.

I close my eyes and give myself five seconds to calm down. Five seconds to accept this and move on.

When I open my eyes, Helen's lips twitch up slightly. She knows she's won this round.

Helen stands and walks around her desk. 'Now that's sorted, let's get you enrolled, shall we?' She opens the door but stops and turns back to us as we stand. 'Ah, before we go, did anyone want to move into the accommodation here?' We all shake our heads. 'I didn't think so.'

She walks out of the door and Janesh and Ivy leave behind her.

Isaac grabs my hand, pulling me back. 'What do you think of the ultimatum?' he asks quietly.

I shrug. 'I didn't trust them already, but now I definitely don't. We need to be careful.'

He nods. 'Yeah, I agree.'

'Isaac, Adelaide?' Helen's voice rings through the corridor outside the office, and we walk out briskly to meet the group.

She takes us down the corridor and around more bends until we find the lecture rooms.

She stops outside a door. 'In here, you'll collect your student cards and log-in details, so you can access your timetables and module guides. You'll find the app is already on your phones.'

I frown, taking out my phone, and unlocking it. Sure enough, the app is now on the menu. I'd assumed they were only checking our texts and calls—like they do with the rest of the country to find rebels. And sure, maybe tracking them, that's why Charmaine always leaves her phone in our flat when she goes out at night. But this feels more intrusive somehow. How much access do they have to our phones? And what else do they have access to? The camera at the top of the phone seems to glare at me.

Once we've got everything sorted, we're told our cars are waiting for us at the entrance and to use the maps on our phones to find our way out of the building.

This entire time, we've ignored Janesh, and I feel a pang of guilt. I hate ignoring people, but he did so many atrocious things—I don't feel like I can forgive him. I glance back at him as we walk, but he won't meet my eye. His shoulders are drooped, and he walks with his hands in his pockets. I feel some sort of sadness for him, even though I know I shouldn't. I know how awful I'd feel if everyone refused to speak to me.

'I think we're going the wrong way,' I say, putting my hand on Isaac to stop him and looking at the map on my phone.

Ivy and Janesh stop behind us.

'It's all one way,' he replies, looking at his own map. He shrugs. 'It'll probably take us longer to go back the way we came.'

It takes us another ten minutes to find the entrance.

As we step out, we finally see other students. Normal students. They're bringing in their belongings, moving in for the first semester of the year. I can't help but watch them all, my mouth turned down, as they embark on something that seems so normal to the outside world; but not to us. I don't know what normal is anymore.

We find three cars waiting for us. The students moving in give us odd looks. I don't know if they recognise us, or if they just think it's weird that we have a personal car service.

I turn my back to them, stopping Ivy before she walks to her car. 'Bit overwhelming, wasn't it?'

'Yeah, exciting though. I didn't finish my degree before loans were scrapped, so I'm looking forward to finally doing that.'

'Yeah, me too, I guess.' I look over my shoulder and see Janesh watching us, he chews on his bottom lip as if he's waiting for the right moment to say something. I turn back to Ivy. 'How are you feeling about studying with Janesh?'

She clenches her jaw, and her eyes dull slightly. 'As long as he stays away from me, we won't have a problem.'

Isaac says from beside me, 'That's something we can all agree on.'

I laugh slightly, but the guilty feeling in my chest won't go away. I try to push it from my mind and give Ivy a small smile.

'You should come over for tea one day after seminars. You can meet my roommate, Charmaine.'

Her eyes light up. 'I'd really like that; I don't have anyone outside of my family to talk to right now.'

'I get it. Give me your phone, and I'll put my number in. Text me whenever you want.' Once I give her the phone back, the driver opens our door for us. 'See you in the morning then.'

'Yeah, see you,' Ivy says, looking across the buildings, and into the distance.

I chew on the inside of my cheek, but don't say anything. We both went through the same trauma. I don't think any of us are really coping with it as well as we think we are. We're hiding it as much as possible, but I know it needs an outlet. I let a breath loose. She'll talk about it when she's ready.

The trip back to our flats seemed quicker than the way to uni, but maybe I just wasn't paying attention. We get out of the car, Isaac joining me at the entrance to our flats. I stop before walking in. Isaac stands straight, facing me but stretching his arms in the air. Two hours in the car is a long time when you're not used to it.

The car drives away, and I stare into the empty woods across the road, my mind occupied about the possibilities of what's to come.

'Hey, I'm gonna go for a walk down to the shops,' I say to Isaac.

'Want some company?' he asks, tilting his head to the side.

I force a smile and give him a peck on the lips. 'I just need to decompress.'

I put my headphones on and walk away without looking back.

Charmaine got me an MP3 player for my birthday back in April. It's filled with all my old favourite songs. I don't know how she got the music for it, considering none of it is on the approved lists, but it made me love her a little bit more.

When I get to the shops, I look around without really seeing anything. With the money provided by the government, I can afford clothes and household items that I used to think of as luxuries. But after furnishing our flat and buying new clothes, I've tried to only shop on the cheaper end. You never know when you might need that extra money.

I end up in a charity shop because the money made here supposedly goes to the orphanages in London, but during the six months we've been down here, I haven't seen any. And I've searched endlessly. I just want to help the people living in them because nobody ever helped me. But they're impossible to find.

I glance over the clothes and the approved books on the shelves, but I don't buy anything.

I leave and go into the corner shop next door. I buy some crisps and chocolate, enough to fill a bag for me and Charmaine. We always keep a cupboard filled with snacks now. They were banned in the orphanage, along with most things, so we occasionally overindulge. Sometimes, our lives feel too good to be true, and we don't want to waste any of these moments. Today proved that we need to keep hold of them.

I leave the shop and walk to the other end of the street to the closest ATM. I look around the area to make sure nobody is watching before taking out three hundred pounds. I try to hide it in front of me as much as possible before slipping it into my purse. My stomach is starting to hurt, and I need to get home quickly. I know I shouldn't be doing this, but it's done now.

Back at the flat, I check my bathroom again for any cameras, but as usual, I find none. I unscrew the siding of the bath, pull it away and reveal the wide, round tub. I put the cash into a plastic bag and put it under the bath, where I've been hiding cash for the last few months. There's every chance I'll need it someday. I replace the siding and flush the toilet, creating some kind of sound to fool those watching the cameras.

I leave the bathroom, shutting the door behind me. The smell of Charmaine's cooking reaches me through the closed door, and I shut my eyes. I can't tell her about any of this, not until I've made a decision about her rebellion.

Is it hers? I shake my head. I don't know anything about it. And right now isn't the time to think about it. I let myself relax for a moment, the thoughts of packing a bag, taking the money, and running so prevalent in my head. I have a way out if I need it. Something I didn't have before.

I'm not trapped.

CHAPTER SIX

I wake the next morning with a weird feeling in my stomach and throat, chasing away the nightmare about Celeste. I pull the sheets under my chin but make no movement to get out of bed. I feel like something bad is going to happen today, which makes sense after Helen's proclamation yesterday. But it feels like more than just that.

There's been a shadow creeping over my happiness for the last six months, and I think it's finally going to show its face.

I stare at the ceiling, willing myself to get out of bed. I just need to sit up, that's all. One step at a time. But it's too hard. I close my eyes tight and rub them with my fists. There, a movement I didn't even think about. I groan. It shouldn't be this difficult. I've wanted to go back to uni for years, what's stopping me now? I mean, besides having the choice of course taken away from me. I'm being ridiculous. I open my eyes and sit up.

My room looks normal. It is normal. *I'm* normal. But I can't shake this feeling, like my stomach is rolling.

I swing my legs over the bed and stretch. I've got this. I push the feeling away; it's still there, lodged in my stomach, but I can ignore it. I'm great at ignoring things.

I take a quick shower, washing my hair and scrubbing my skin red. It takes a while to force myself to leave the safety of the hot water. But I do. Wrapping a towel around my hair, then a bigger one around my body, I walk back into my bedroom and to my wardrobe. Would it be too cliché to go full academia with my outfit? Maybe I'm too old for the look. I turned twenty-four at the end of April, so I'm not nearly thirty, but I'm closer to that age than I am to sixteen. I shudder, the thought of getting to thirty and still being limited on freedom is something I can't quite stomach right now.

Fuck it, I can wear what I want. I can *afford* to wear what I want.

I pull out a dark green tartan skirt, a long-sleeved black turtleneck jumper, and some black tights. I dress quickly, and then French plait my hair back to keep it off my face.

I pick up a black, leather satchel bag, and black Doc Marten boots. I think it's still too warm for a full coat, so I put on a fake leather jacket and head into the kitchen. It's ten to eight, and the car will be here soon. The kitchen is tidy, the flat cold and quiet. Either Charmaine is already out, doing whatever she does now on her days off, or she's still asleep. I grab a banana on my way out of the flat, eating it once I get in the lift.

On the way out of the building, I nod to the security official by the door and drop the banana peel in the bin. Isaac is already waiting outside. Like me, it seems he chose to look slightly academic in his slate shirt and black jeans. He's even tucked the shirt in, though he's left the collar loose, and pulled his sleeves up so his forearms show. I bite my lip, allowing myself one second of fantasy. It involves him and I on a desk, and I think we're going to have to act it out soon.

He sees my look as I walk over to him and his eyes darken, making my cheeks flush. 'What's that look about?' he asks.

'You'll see tonight,' I say with a smile.

'Don't do that to me.' He kisses me deeply, before resting his forehead against mine. 'What if I can't wait until tonight?'

From the corner of my eye, I see the car pulling up, and I smile. 'You're going to have to, I'm afraid. Unless you want to traumatise our driver?'

'Today will be painful,' he laughs.

His laughter softens some of the dread I feel.

'The only thing you need to know about me is that I take no shit,' Professor Adcock says. His first name is Ryan, but he says we can't use that unless we want lower marks. I doubt he has the authority to do that, but whatever. He's a small balding man who seems to have a permanent frown on his face. 'If you're late to my class, miss one, or need an extension, it must be a life-or-death situation. Otherwise, you have no excuse. Understood?'

The class nods.

There are just under thirty of us in the lecture hall. The Professor stands at the front, behind a lectern and in front of an interactive whiteboard with "*Introduction to Politics*" written on it.

Professor Adcock continues, 'For half of the day, you'll be in a lecture learning about Politics in the Modern World, in the afternoon you'll be starting your practice-based assignment, which will be assessed before Christmas break. You will also sit an exam when you return in January. Any questions?'

Other students shift in their seats, but most stay quiet.

I grip my pen in my hand. I've always been bad at exams about anything other than science and literature. I don't know how I'm going to pass this. Then again, I managed to pass the exam to get into the trials, but I was enthusiastic about it then. When I didn't know the truth. I clench my jaw, now isn't the time to think about that.

One person puts his hand up. Janesh.

'What is the practice-based assignment?' he asks.

The professor cocks an eyebrow. 'What's your name?'

'Janesh, sir.'

'Ah, one of the trials' winners. How nice to have someone on this course with real life experience.' I roll my eyes. Yeah, experience in being an absolute dick. 'This isn't the time to talk about your assignments, you'll find that out when you separate into your groups.'

Janesh just nods eagerly. From the corner of my eye, I see Isaac cringe. Janesh becoming a teacher's pet is as unbelievable to him as it is to me.

Nobody else raises their hand, so the professor goes on. 'You will be split into two groups. Those with surnames beginning with A to M will have their practice-based groups in the morning and lectures in the afternoon, and vice versa for those with surnames beginning with N to Z.' That means me and Isaac can stay together at least, and Ivy will be in our group, too. It also means avoiding Janesh. Some tension from my shoulders eases and I relax a little. 'The first group will be able to leave when we break for lunch, but you'll have an extra day at the end of term, the second group will go to room 11b after lunch.'

When the lecture is over, my brain feels fried from all the first day information. I pack my bag away, putting my new course book inside, and search for Ivy. She's a few rows in front of us, and her hair stands out amongst a group of brunettes. She's dyed it a bubble gum pink. Our eyes connect, and she gives me a small smile before rushing to join us.

'So, lunch?' she asks.

My stomach grumbles in answer. 'I am ruled by my stomach, please lead the way.'

The queue in the main campus canteen is relatively short, it looks like only our politics class are here still. Are there no other classes at this university? I don't know how many people actually go to university anymore now it's only open to the wealthy, though.

A sign above the counter shows the daily food menu, including what they serve for breakfast. I might have to ask our driver to pick us up ten minutes earlier, if it means I don't have to worry about breakfast from now on.

Spoilt for choice, I choose a spinach and falafel cheeseburger with chips. It's been eight months since I left the orphanage, but I still worry I'm taking too much. It's amazing how much choice you can have with some semblance of freedom. We choose a round table at the back, though with it being so empty, we could sit anywhere. I take a bite of my food and marvel at how great it tastes. When I was at uni before, it was always overcooked and hard, but not this. The cheese is melted perfectly, and the bun is toasted just right so it's not falling apart.

I'm so engrossed in the burger that I don't realise Isaac and Ivy have been having a conversation.

Isaac is smirking, and I have to blink a few times, to realise he's just said something to me. I swallow a chunk of the burger.

'What was that?' I ask.

'That burger must be really good,' he says. 'I just said we're really glad we don't have to be with Janesh all term. Right?'

'Sorry,' I say, gulping down the last bite of my burger. 'That burger was euphoric. But yeah, you're right. I don't have to go through my day feeling guilty.'

'What would you have to feel guilty about?' Ivy says, scowling. 'You didn't do anything to *him.*'

'I can't help but feel guilty when I ignore someone. It's fine.' I shake my head, as if I'm removing the thought from my mind. 'I'm sure it'll pass.'

I pick at my chips as they continue their conversation.

'Hey, Ivy,' I say when I finish. 'I really love this new hair colour.'

She beams at me. 'Really? I wasn't sure about it at all.'

I nod. 'Really.'

'I don't think I'll keep it, though. Now I can afford hair dye, I think I'll keep changing it.'

My face softens. 'Yeah, I'd probably do the same. This is my virgin colour though; I don't know if I'd ever get it back. Or if anything else would suit me.'

Isaac wipes a crumb from the corner of my mouth. 'You'd look perfect no matter what.'

Ivy rolls her eyes, which makes me laugh. 'Sorry, we're still in the honeymoon phase.'

Her shoulders slump. 'It's fine. I'm just jealous I never got to do any of this with Violet.'

I can't believe I didn't think of that. They never had the chance to have a normal relationship. Of course she'd be grieving that. And here we are flaunting ours in front of her.

'I'm sorry, Ivy,' Isaac says.

She shrugs and twirls some spaghetti around her fork. 'It's fine. I'm not going to stop you two being happy.' She looks up with a sad smile on her face. 'Someone should be after what we went through.'

Before I can answer, my phone beeps with a reminder for our next class. The sound echoes through the room. We all start packing away and standing to leave.

Ivy shrugs and we all make our way around the building to our next room. Unlike the lecture hall, the room is all one level with single desks pushed together, making four bigger squares.

'Before you all sit down,' Professor Adcock says. 'I'd like you to form four groups of three.'

Besides me, there are eleven others in our class, mixed genders, meaning four groups. Most of the students are fresh out of A levels, some even seem to know each other. Maybe they're roommates, I don't know. A few of them glance back at us, they know who we are but won't approach us for whatever reason. Maybe it's obvious we'll stay together.

I see one girl stood at the front, her arms hiding her body, crumpling her tartan dress. She doesn't know where to go.

She doesn't have to wait long as two girls who know each other walk over with a smile and ask her to join their group. This all happens within about thirty seconds.

Isaac and Ivy both look at me. It's obvious we're not going to split up, and nobody else tries to invite us into their groups.

We choose one of the two sets of desks at the back and take our places. I take out a notepad and pen. I could use the tablet I was given when I moved into my new home, but I've never really liked typing on it. Others around the room take out personal laptops. I don't know why I didn't think of that.

Professor Adcock coughs from the front of the room.

'This afternoon, we'll be discussing what your practical assignment will be,' he says. 'Please leave all questions to the end.'

He switches the interactive whiteboard on. A PowerPoint presentation fills the screen.

The rest of the room falls away and my stomach drops. All I can see are the words written on the screen: "*The Trials*."

We're being sent back in. Somehow, we've broken the law, and this class was just a ploy to catch us all.

Every single moment of the trials comes back to me within seconds. Brett being dragged away into the night, Angus trying to kill me, Heather dying next to me just from the touch of a plant. The obstacle course. The escape room and Celeste.

Not Celeste. I push her from my mind, but she's replaced by the memory of Thomas; his beheading becoming forefront. I can't go through this again.

A small chatter echoes through the room. Everyone else is panicking, too, surely. I look at Isaac. His jaw is clenched, and his fists are gripped so hard that his knuckles are turning white. I put a hand over one of his, he looks at me, his face is clouded with anger. My eyes widen and I shake my head to tell him I have no idea what is going on either.

Professor Adcock coughs, and the chatter dies down. 'No, you're not going into the trials,' he chuckles. 'No. This is different.'

I breathe a sigh of relief. But that's quickly knocked from me.

He continues, 'Each group will be planning two stages of the trials each. Mock trials, that is,' Professor Adcock says with a chuckle. 'The next lot starts in four months, it's far too late to start planning it now. The looks on some of your faces, honestly. You'd think we were actually sending you into them!' He looks up at Ivy, Isaac, and I and his face falls. 'Ah, yes. Well, we do have some trial winners in here with us who know first-hand how it actually feels to be in the trials. I don't know why the rest of you look like you have any idea. You don't. Just make sure you don't commit any crimes and you won't ever have to learn. Now, how this will work is...'

I tune him out. He can't be serious, right? I'm sure everyone else must be fine with designing a new set of trials. But mock or not, I don't ever want to relive them. I'm not even planning on watching the next ones. I don't want anything to do with them. I can't speak for the other three, even Janesh, but I bet they don't either. I find myself raising my hand without thinking.

Professor Adcock pauses, looking over to me. 'Adelaide, is it?' I nod. 'Please leave all questions until the end.'

'But—'

'No, whatever you have to say can wait.' He continues his speech.

I'm not even sure what it is I wanted to say. I can't back out without losing everything. I might as well be back in the trials.

'You'll each be designing two trials per group. Overall, there will be eight.'

No. *No.* How can they do this? Are they purposefully trying to torture us? What does any of this have to do with politics? My eyes blur and tears threaten to spill. I can hear Celeste's joyful laugh, lost to the world thanks to the type of trials I now have to plan. How can I do that to someone else?

I take a deep breath.

I'm not. He said *mock* trials. I'm not putting anyone through anything. This is just to prepare us for future trials in case we go into that branch of government. I can't see myself going into any of the branches, but that doesn't matter right now. What matters is getting through this semester. Through planning fake trials. They have to be, there's no way they'd put us through it all again. We're just first year uni students, we have no power here. They wouldn't let us plan something that's so important to them.

I can plan mock trials. I'm sure I can.

'The first set of trials drew in a huge audience, almost the entire country watched. It was voted the top show of the year,' he cringes, showing he has a little decency.

I feel like I can't breathe.

Show? Killing and torturing us all was just entertainment for these arseholes.

We weren't criminals. But they don't deserve that. I don't even know why some of us were chosen. Maybe they were weeding out the poor. But then, how did someone like Brett get through? My mum would tell me to stop. Think. Process and listen. But it's so hard not to question everything. She said that was one of the things she loved most about me, but also one of the most frustrating. I just can't let anything lie.

Questions are asked at the end of the lecture, but I don't raise my hand again. There's nothing I could ask to make this better. The rest of the students are mostly curious about how far they need to go with the planning. I don't really care.

We leave the building at the end of the day with no new information, just that we will begin tomorrow, and we must all decide as a team what our trials will be. I don't even want to think about it, to prepare. But our homework is to each come up with a theme for the entire thing.

Isaac and I don't speak on the drive home, both processing what we're being forced to do.

I try to say my mantra. *My name is Adelaide Taylor, and I will not let them break me.*

But I feel like I'm letting them do just that. My worst fears are real, and I can no longer evade them.

CHAPTER SEVEN

The ceiling in my new bedroom has glow-in-the-dark stars stuck to it. I lie on the bed with the lights off, staring at them, staring through them, as if I can see the real night sky. But you can't see the stars here in London. Even with less cars, less pollution in the atmosphere, down here it's all still ruined.

When I was ten, my dad took me on a camping trip near Castleton. It was so hot during the summer it felt like the sky was on fire. He let me stay up late so he could show me each one of the constellations. At the time, I thought Taurus would be my favourite, being my star sign and all, but I was disappointed to find that it didn't really look like a bull. No, my favourite was Orion. The way it looked like it was dancing made me feel alive. My dad got us up from the ground and we danced in silence, the stars were our own kind of music.

Since that day, whenever I look at the sky and see Orion, I think of my dad, and I know he's up there dancing. I can still picture it so clearly and a smile tugs at my lips.

The stars above me come into view, having blurred out during my memory, and my smile dims. I don't know when I'll be able to see the clear night sky and Orion again. I don't know if I'll ever hear their music, or dance like I once did. Young and free, with no responsibilities, and nothing to worry about. When my future still held promises and hopes of my own; before it was all taken away from me.

And now, here I lie in a bedroom given to me by a government I hate who are controlling every part of my life. I'll never be young and free again.

***

My eyes spring open as Charmaine forces herself into my room and turns the big light on. I didn't even realise I'd fallen asleep for a few hours. Or that I'd done it without having to turn the bathroom light on. I must have been exhausted. I didn't have any nightmares.

The light burns and I put my arm over my eyes.

'No, take the ghastly thing away, please, I beg of you,' I say.

Charmaine laughs and does as I say, walking over to the bed and laying down next to me. 'Sorry, didn't realise you'd turned into a creature of darkness.'

'I didn't even realise I'd fallen asleep. I usually have the bathroom light on.'

'Does it remind you of the orphanage?' She nudges me and I remove my arm from my eyes.

'That, and the trials. I used to love laying in the dark after a full day of uni. Now it just brings back nightmares. The Madame didn't help either, taking the choice away from us.'

Even with all the money she had coming in from the women in our house, the Madame still claimed she couldn't afford electric bills and forced us into darkness each night. It was worse during the basement punishments when we'd get locked down there in the cold. With no windows, our eyes had to adjust, we'd often see dark figures moving around. I still don't know if it was my imagination.

Charmaine sighs. 'Well, at least you have the freedom to choose things now.' I bristle at her words and turn stiff. 'What? What did I say?'

'Nothing. It's just, we're not really free, are we? This,' I gesture around the room. 'This could be taken away at any moment if I step out of line.' I breathe out a sigh. 'It became very clear today that I never really escaped the trials.'

Charmaine turns onto her side and watches me watching the ceiling. 'Addy. What happened today?'

I close my eyes and run a hand down my face. I sit up and lean against the wooden headboard, fairy lights poking into my back. But I don't care. The pain focuses me.

'You're not going to like it,' I say.

She shrugs. 'Tell me anyway.'

I sigh. 'They're making us plan mock trials. If we don't do it, then we're off the course and we lose everything.' Tears threaten to consume me, and I clench my teeth, willing anger to take over from the grief.

'And you're just going along with it?' Charmaine asks, sitting up and crossing her legs.

'What choice do I have?' I say, throwing my hands up. 'Like I said, if I don't do it, we'll lose everything.'

'What about Celeste? What would she think to all of this?'

I shrink back. I knew she'd say something like that, poking at my weak spots to get the reaction she wants.

'Don't,' I say.

'Don't what?'

'Don't bring her into this.'

She throws her hands up in exasperation. 'Addy, don't you see what they're doing? They've taken *your* worst nightmare and they've made it your entire life. I bet this won't affect the other three as much. But you, I can see you're on the verge of tears just thinking about it.'

I take a deep breath, calming myself before I speak. 'It's not real.'

'What?'

'The trials. They're not real. We just have to pretend they are.'

She looks at me in disbelief. 'You can't honestly believe that, can you?'

'It's September, Charmaine, the next trials start in January. There's no way they're not already prepared for them.'

'They can do anything as quickly as they want, and they're using you so they don't have to plan them. They're pushing you to see how far they can go before you break. I can't believe you don't see it.'

I shake my head. 'They have no reason to do that. They already have us trapped. This is just my future. It's fine. I'm fine. I can cope.'

I tell her so I can tell myself. Saying it out loud makes it almost believable.

'You're lying to yourself, and you know it.' She shakes her head and begins turning away. She stops, her eyes lighting up like she's just got an idea. 'Actually, this is perfect. This is exactly what we need.'

'What are you talking about?'

Charmaine looks up at the corners of the room, at the small cameras trying so hard to hide themselves from us. 'What I spoke to you about when we moved in. This is what we need. You could really help us.'

I groan. 'Oh, Charmaine, not this again. For God's sake, how many times do I have to tell you that I haven't made a decision yet?'

'You're going to have to. And soon. Before they use you more. This is it, Addy! Don't you see? We can use this—'

I put my hand up. 'Stop. I've had enough.'

'Addy, come on, we—'

I get off the bed. 'There is no "we" Charmaine, why can't you see that? I'm not risking everything by helping you out. So, drop it, okay?'

Charmaine stands, crossing her arms and jutting out her chin. 'I won't, Addy. I'll never drop it. You just need to see what we can do. Come to a meeting, talk to everyone. That will convince you, I promise.'

'NO.' She shrinks back at my voice, but I can't take it anymore, I've had enough. I grab a bag out of my cupboard and start to pack. 'I'm staying at Isaac's tonight. Don't follow me and don't try calling me.'

She glares at me. 'Fine, but you're making a mistake by not listening to me.'

I roll my eyes. 'Well, it's my mistake to make.'

I storm out of the flat and across the hall to Isaac's. He opens the door on my fifth knock, too eager to get away from Charmaine to stop.

'What's wrong?' he asks, his eyebrows furrowing in confusion. The tears I held back come rushing out and he opens his arms to me. 'Oh, Addy, what happened?'

I don't speak, I just sob into his jumper, and he closes the door behind me.

'It's the mock trials, isn't it?' he asks, rubbing my back. 'I know. It's going to be hard, but we can do this. I promise you.' He tilts my head up to look at him, his eyes searching for something, but I don't know what. 'I'm here, you've got me, and you won't lose me. We've already proven we can survive as long as we have each other. So that's what we'll keep doing. Surviving.'

The tears slow and I reach up, hooking a hand behind his neck and bringing his lips down to mine. He kisses me softly, slowly, and I push my body against his.

Carefully, he removes his mouth from mine. 'Addy, is this a good idea right now?'

I stop crying and smile slightly. 'I just want a break from feeling like this. I need to feel something else. Feeling *you* would be nice.'

He chuckles. 'Well how can I say no to that.' He pushes his lips against mine, hard for a moment, but soon breaks away again. 'But we'll talk later?'

I just nod, kissing him again as we back towards his bedroom.

'Actually,' I say, stopping him, remembering the fantasy from this morning. 'What about your office?'

His eyes darken as he grabs my hand and pulls me into the next room. He turns to shut the door and I undress quickly, jumping backwards onto his desk. I widen my legs before him, leaning back. He crosses his arms, watching me as I play with my peaked nipple before dipping my hand lower, deep down to my core, to the wetness only Isaac can make happen. I run my hand along myself without breaking eye contact, and lift my fingers to my mouth, tasting myself. Isaac swallows, his Adam's apple bobbing, and walks across to me. He takes my hand from my mouth, gripping both of my wrists and holding them against the desk.

'Let me,' he says and lowers in front of me.

His mouth finds me ready for him, and he chuckles against me, making me tremble.

He tastes me, taking his time, yet still giving me release too quickly.

I pant as he stands before me, pining for more. He undresses, letting me eye his impressive length. I almost beg but stop myself, biting my bottom lip.

He leans over me again. 'Let me do that too,' he says, and I let my lip go.

He kisses me deeply, pulling my bottom lip between his teeth. He slips inside me and fucks me harder and faster than he ever has before, gripping my hips. Tidal waves of pleasure course through me. He stops and slips out, neither of us finished. He pulls me off the desk. I raise my eyebrows at him, but he just turns me around and bends me over the desk.

'Have I ever told you that your ass is perfect?' I shake my head. 'I'm normally a boob guy, and God, I love yours, but your ass. Fuck me. I could stare at it all day long.'

My heart quickens as he stands behind me, his hand circling.

A sharp sting slaps against my ass cheek. Pain and pleasure ripples through me and I look back at Isaac.

'Do that again,' I say.

He smirks, but does as I say, as he makes me groan in pleasure once more. He rubs his cock over my wetness, making me take a sharp breath.

'Please,' I groan, and he chuckles.

He pushes into me, and I feel myself squeeze around his length.

'You make me insatiable, Adelaide,' he says as he pulls out and slams into me again.

I move my hips back, meeting him with every thrust. He groans my name, and a shiver of pleasure goes through me. This man could destroy me, and I'd let him.

We both collapse in utter ecstasy. He lays against my back, both of us covered in sweat.

'Let's go to bed,' he breathes against my neck.

'I'm not ready to sleep.'

He chuckles, pulling me up and turning me around. He pinches my ass.

'That's not what I had in mind.'

We go into his bedroom, both lying in bed, facing each other.

His eyes search my face. 'What are you thinking?'

'That I don't want this to ever end.'

He frowns. 'It doesn't have to. I'm not going anywhere.'

I shrug, looking at my hands. 'I just don't think I can lose you.'

He pulls me towards him, leaning his forehead against mine. 'You won't. I'm here for the long run, I promise.'

I smile slightly. 'You might just ruin me,' I say, raising a hand to his face, stroking along the stubble and he cocks his head, frowning. 'I don't mean that in a bad way,' I add quickly. 'I just mean that I'm yours. Completely. I hope you know that.'

He closes his eyes and breathes out, almost like a sigh of relief. 'And I'm yours, Addy. It's always going to be you.'

He kisses me slowly, lifting my leg up to his hip before pushing inside me.

We make love—a word I'm still not ready to use. But I'm getting there. I think he is, too.

Isaac's fingers trail along my spine, waking me up, making every part of me tingle.

'Careful,' I say. 'I'll never get out of bed if you keep doing that.'

Isaac chuckles. 'Wouldn't want that now, would we?'

His hands dip lower, and I can't contain the shiver that goes through me. 'Isaac,' I groan.

'I love it when you say my name like that.'

'Come on,' I say pushing him slightly. 'We have to get up.'

He sighs heavily and removes his hand. 'I know. Do you want to tell me what happened last night?'

I rub the back of my neck, my heart fluttering thinking about what happened. 'Not really. Charmaine and I had an argument about the mock trials. She thinks they'll be real and I'm a fool for returning.'

'She might be right,' he says, and I shoot a glare at him. He puts his hands up defensively.

'Hey now, I said *might*. We're both fools for staying, but we also know we can't leave. And that's okay for now.'

I nod against his chest. 'For now.'

'Do you want to go and talk to Charmaine before we leave?'

I shake my head. 'I'll talk to her later. I need to get through the day without her guilt tripping me. Besides,' I say with a sigh. 'I never did my homework.'

Isaac grimaces. 'No, me neither.'

'So, what should we suggest, what can our grand idea for the trials be?'

'It's not going to be just one and done, is it? It'll be a series of them.'

'Yeah, Adcock said we need to come up with an overall theme.'

'What theme?'

It's so horrible to even have to think of a way to kill people. I tried so hard all night to not think about it, but I couldn't rest my mind. I tried to think of horror movies, in the hopes that using something fake would make it feel less like the actual trials. And one subgenre kept circling my mind.

'I'm thinking of the horror movies from the late twenty-tens. Do you remember the horror attraction ones?'

His eyes light up with a smile. 'Not really, I was never a fan of them.'

'Well, characters would go out on Halloween, and they'd find either a horror-themed fairground, or signs for a warehouse promising something "fun". I think that's what we need to do.'

'A funhouse of horror? Except someone dies in each room?'

I grimace. 'Sort of. It needs to be bigger. An entire horror festival with different attractions with death around every corner.' I stare at nothing, picturing what's to come, who they might make us. 'I think this could break us.'

Isaac nods and pulls me towards his chest. 'At least we'll be together.'

And so, the trials begin.

CHAPTER EIGHT

P rofessor Adcock chooses our horror attraction theme for the trials, and every group gets two trials each to conceive. With four groups that means there will be eight trials, two more than we had to go through. More chances for death. *If they were real,* I tell myself, *and they're not, so you need to relax.* But I can't. I chew on the inside of my cheek until it draws blood, distracting myself.

We're given the first trial, horror attraction, whatever you want to call it, and Ivy decides it'll be a train, taking the participants to the attractions. The "Horror Express", she's calling it, making me grimace. Everyone wakes up on bunks, not knowing how they got there, like we did at the beginning of our trials. And then the horror commences.

We need to make another attraction as well; it can be anywhere as there wouldn't be a specific path for the fake participants to take and they could go to any attraction as they see fit.

It takes us weeks to figure something out.

During that time, we become closer to Ivy. She grieved for a while after the trials, for her girlfriend, for who she used to be. She told us about her nightmares. They're like mine but mostly about Violet. She sees the arrow protruding from her eye almost nightly. She chose not to sleep for a while, but that just made her mind run wilder. The anxiety from sleep deprivation made her paranoid, and she couldn't even be around her family for a long time. She thought everyone was out to get her.

But she's decided now that she's been gifted. She's trying to see the rewards for winning the trials as just that. Not as the control we're under. She hopes this is freedom.

'What about Janesh?' I ask during one of our lunch breaks.

She looks up, scratching at her shoulder. 'What about him?'

I shift in my seat, regretting that I'm bringing him up. 'What he did to us all in the trials. What he did to Violet.'

She stiffens at Violet's name. Noticing her reaction, she leans back in her chair, trying to appear as relaxed as she can. 'That's his problem. I don't forgive him, but I don't want to give any energy into holding a grudge.'

As if he heard his name, I see him lift his head to us and meet my eyes from across the room. He begins to stand, but I shake my head and he sits back down, his shoulders slumping—defeated. Maybe I should take the same approach as Ivy. I know he had his reasons for what he did, he'll never forget them just as we'll never forget the trials. He's responsible for at least three deaths: Angus, Heather, and Violet. The last one completely by his own hands. Each death provides their own brand of trauma for us all, I'm certain that includes him. I'm just not ready to let him in yet. He needs to live with what he did. Just as we all do.

And so, we move on, all of us. Sort of. We're distracted if nothing else.

Our entire focus becomes learning the intricacies of our course in the mornings and planning the fake trials in the afternoon. We don't know what the other groups, both in this class and the morning one, are planning. But we do know that there'll be a vote on the best overall. I don't know if I'd want to be called the best at planning someone's murder.

It's our Thursday afternoon class, and we're all tapping away on our tablets. I click on my Facebook and go through my old photos.

I stop at a photo from a Sunday where Charmaine and I had a day off together and decided to go and walk around the area, away from the orphanage. The Madame gave us permission, I still don't know why. She would always give us extra chores around the house on our days off; she must have been in one of her very rare good moods that day.

Anyway, the photo is of me and Charmaine stood underneath a Willow tree near an unused tram stop. I'd walk past it with my dad when I was a kid and I had told her about how I used to want to live under the branches, the leaves giving me all the protection I needed. She had laughed and we made it our new place to go whenever we had a spare moment. That same day, we walked up the road and found the psychiatric hospital turned flats, which is now abandoned.

We're a couple of weeks into planning. Our first trial is planned, it just needs refining. Ivy is coming over tonight to get that done for tomorrow.

I straighten in my seat and put my tablet down, speaking for the first time in twenty minutes.

'What if our second trial is a building rather than an attraction,' I say.

Isaac and Ivy look up from their tablets. After a few weeks, none of us have come up with any concrete ideas. We just don't have enough heart to put in it. It's only because I'd been thinking about that day, that the idea even came to me.

'Go on,' Isaac says.

'When I lived in Sheffield, we had an abandoned psychiatric hospital near our house,' I say, remembering the time Charmaine and I ventured too close and ran away at the first sound. 'It was turned into flats, but before that it was one of the most haunted places in the city. It's where the worst of the worst were sent at the end of the 1900s. Before that, people from World War Two were sent there. From what I've read, it was a horrible place to work for the staff. Not just because of the violent patients, but the ghostly experiences they had. Anyway, there's different stories of small things happening there. So, what if we did that, but upped the horror.'

They both nod so I continue, 'So each room could trap them in it until they find the key. Like an escape room.' I cringe, hating myself for suggesting it after what happened to Celeste. The sound of water fills my ears as my mind tries to take me back to her death, but I close my eyes and breathe slowly in and out. Once I've calmed myself down and the sounds of the room replaces the water, I keep going, finally having some momentum. 'But one could have children's handprints on the ceiling, and the ghost kids could start messing with them, and then another could have an actual patient strapped to the table. Dead or not, but it would move and freak them out.'

'No offense, Addy, but it doesn't sound that scary,' Isaac says, reaching for my hand.

I roll my eyes. 'I know, right now it doesn't. But it's not always what happens in a haunted building that's scary, is it? It's the anticipation.'

Ivy is typing on her tablet and chews on her lips. She puts the tablet down and speaks, 'So I've been researching different plants and what they'd do if they got into our system. Like with Heather and the Wolfsbane.' I wince, remembering sleeping next to her long after she'd died. Ivy gives me a sympathetic look. 'Sorry. I just thought it could be worth looking into. So, I've found this plant called Datura. It's sort of like LSD or mushrooms in that it gives hallucinations. It can be fatal, but if we get the dosage right it shouldn't be and then the hallucinations will help with the fear.'

'I've never even heard of it,' I say.

'Neither had I until now. Back in the early 2000s, teenagers used to take it and there's still some research into it available. I say we use that.'

'It's a bit risky if we don't get the dosage right, but I agree. Now let's plan each room.'

We let Ivy draw the building and then the layout. She'd originally wanted to study architecture but obviously that choice has been taken from her. I wonder if she'll be able to do it in the future if she gets a well enough paid job to pay for the course herself. If we're not forced into careers that is.

The end of the day comes quicker than usual as we've actually had something to do for a change. We all pile out of the front of the uni where our car waits for us, Ivy gets into the front seat while Isaac and I sit in the back.

Charmaine is waiting for us when we get home. Since our last fight, things have been more subdued. We're still best friends, but there's an edge to everything we say. Like she wants to say more but doesn't want to make me mad. Which I get, I don't want to make her mad by saying no again. Not when I still don't have a decision for her. Not when I still haven't told Isaac about it. We promised not to lie to each other, and I'm not doing that intentionally. I just need him to be safe. I don't know what will happen when I do tell him. *When* not *if.*

. He knows I'll tell him when I'm ready. But I don't know if I'll ever be ready. And I need to stop thinking about it.

We order Chinese food and dig in while we type up both trials. Both planned out in full, somehow. This afternoon was the quickest we've ever managed to work, but now we have a rhythm, and we know each other more, it's easier to do it all.

'So, Ivy, where are you from originally? Not London, right?' Charmaine asks.

Ivy raises an eyebrow, pushing her laptop away. 'Can't you tell?'

Charmaine shrugs. 'I mean, you've got a bit of an accent and I know some stuff about you from watching the trials on TV.' Ivy stills. Sometimes it's easy to forget that nothing we went through was private. 'But you never said where you're from.'

Ivy tilts her head to the side. 'Liverpool.'

Charmaine taps at her chin, trying to work Ivy out. 'Your accent isn't that strong.'

'I've moved around a lot.'

Charmaine raises an eyebrow. 'Why?'

'Oh, you know,' Ivy says, flicking her hand dramatically. 'Before I had to move back in with my family by law, I was always meeting the next love of my life and moving across the country to live with them. Girls rush relationships.'

'Don't I know it,' Charmaine says under her breath, and they share a look, a twinkle in both of their eyes.

I raise my eyebrows at Isaac, and he just shrugs as if to say let them do what they want. So, I do, and I clear everything away. I put all the containers in the bin and put the pots in the dishwasher. When I turn back to the living room, Ivy and Charmaine are sat together on the sofa, deep in conversation.

'Ivy, are you good here? I think we're going to bed,' I say, looking at the clock. It's well past eleven now and we still have to be at uni in the morning. The last Friday before reading week, we get to hand in our assignments and get a small reprieve from all the information.

Charmaine rolls her eyes. 'She's fine, Addy. Go get some sleep. Or don't,' she says with a wink. 'I'll call Ivy a car when she's ready to go.'

'Alright then.'

Isaac and I head out of the flat and across to his. Giving ourselves as much privacy as possible.

Over the next week and a half, Ivy is over a lot—spending time with Charmaine. Sometimes they're just talking, sometimes they go out, but more often than not, I find them huddled together on the sofa.

I know Ivy is entitled to move on, but I feel like I've hardly seen Charmaine. Did she have to move on with my best friend?

I chastise myself. She's not taking her away from me, and I'm getting jealous for no reason.

On the Sunday before we go back to uni, Charmaine and I are watching TV, so I decide to ask her about it. 'So, what's going on with you and Ivy, then?'

Her cheeks darken in a blush, and she doesn't meet my eyes. 'Oh, you know, I really like her.' I start to speak, but she interrupts me. 'Don't start. I know it's fast but look at you and Isaac.'

'You know that's different. We were in a life-or-death situation and *then* we decided to take things slower. God, we'd been together for six months before we even had sex.'

'Yeah, you're right, it *is* different. But all relationships are.' She shrugs. 'I like Ivy and I think she likes me, so I just want to see where it goes.'

'Fair enough. Just be careful, she might be more vulnerable after the trials.'

She rolls her eyes. 'Look, this is the first hint of feeling I've had since my parents were deported. I'm being careful. Believe me.'

'Good. And I'm here for both of you if you need to talk about anything. Or if you decide she's going to join your extracurricular activities.'

She laughs. 'Yeah, I don't know about that.' But she won't look at me as she says it and my stomach churns with suspicion.

I drop it. It's not my business.

It's nice that Ivy is finding happiness, gaining a second chance. I think that's what we all need. Including Janesh. I sigh heavily.

'Welcome back, first years. I hope you all enjoyed your breaks,' Professor Adcock says as we all find our seats. There are extra tables set out today. 'Now you've all handed in your assignments, we'll be combining your classes.'

The morning class walks into the room in their groups. A group of guys start pushing each other and laughing about some inside joke, but I tune them out. Nobody has gone out of their way to talk to us in the two months we've been here. Not that we've tried that hard either.

The remaining seats are taken, chairs dragging along the floor, screeching, and making me flinch. Janesh looks around before meeting my stare. I give him a small smile and his eyes widen, shocked at the slight friendliness. But I decided last night that I can't hate him forever. And I want to know why he did what he did. So, I'll be friendly, but I won't make friends.

Professor Adcock claps his hands, bringing us all to attention.

'Now onto the real fun,' he says with a smirk. 'In order for us to pick the best set of trials, we must test each one.'

I stiffen. *What?* I can't believe it. We can't do that. We can't be put into trials, fake or not, they were designed to kill people. Or maim at the very least. This is cruelty, not even just to those of us who survived the first trials, but to the rest of the class. It has to be illegal. Why do they even need to test them? They'll never be used. Bile fills my throat, and I ignore what my subconscious is trying to tell me.

Other class members start to raise their voices in protest. I start to speak, ready to disagree to the assignment, too, when Helen walks into the room. I shrink back into my chair. It can't be good if she's here.

'Quiet everyone,' she says loudly, but without shouting. The class does as she says, those who stood up find their seats again. 'You won't be participating in trials. You don't have to worry about that.' She smirks slightly. 'No, we've found that you're all worthy of doing this course. And in fact, some of you are incredibly inventive.' She looks at our group as she says this.

It was just fake as far as we knew, why *wouldn't* we be inventive?

'Yes, quite,' Professor Adcock says and defers to Helen again.

She gives him a small smile before continuing, 'As you know, the first trials were a practice run themselves. With volunteers from around the country,' she says, looking at all of us winners in turn. 'The next set of trials, beginning in January, two months from now, will also be volunteers of a kind. Any criminals committing a crime lesser than rape or terrorism, between the ages of eighteen and twenty-five will be given a choice: execution or entering the trials. Of course, they won't all make it past the written exams or the training. But some will.' She looks around the room, knowing she has every single student listening to her. 'So, what do we do with those over twenty-five? They'll still be executed, yes. But before that, they deserve a proper punishment. More than the prison system can give them.'

Students around the room murmur or nod in agreement. I shake my head slightly, my mouth dropping in shock. The people here are callous, I knew that when they had no problem designing trials, but agreeing to further punishment, especially when some of the so-called criminals are executed without any proof given to the public of their crimes. They could be innocent for all we know. Isaac's hand finds mine and grips it tightly. My stomach tightens, I don't think she's told us the worst of what is to come yet.

Helen nods, noticing the agreement around the room and ignoring my group. 'Yes, they are criminals after all. The dregs of society, hardly worth a trial. Well, not your usual kind anyway,' she says with a smile. 'No. We've decided that a handful of the criminals currently sitting in our overcrowded prisons awaiting execution *will* have a trial. Your trials to be exact. We'll be putting them in your mock trials and seeing how well they survive. And then we'll pick the best eight.'

She pauses, taking in the quiet of the room, waiting to see if anyone objects before she drops the worst of what she's going to say. What my brain has been trying to warn me of that I couldn't accept. What I still can't accept.

Her eyes twinkle, she knows she has everyone, she can feel the excited buzz sparking the room, just as I can. And then she drops it.

'The best eight will be used in January. In the second annual trials.'

CHAPTER NINE

I've never believed in the death penalty. Even for murderers. How does killing someone for their crimes make us any better than them? And the lesser crimes: the rebels, the thieves, the people in the wrong place at the wrong time. How do they deserve to be put to death? Executed live on TV as a warning for the rest of the population.

Since leaving the trials and watching myself the first night, I've barely watched the news, not wanting to see all the bad things happening in the country. It might make me ignorant, but I've already seen too much death in my twenty-four years on this planet.

And now I'm going to have a hand in the death myself. I hope to God we didn't make them good enough to be chosen. At least then the death I cause will be limited.

But we're still going to be killing those deemed criminals in the practice trials to see if they're worthy of the choice. And what will happen to those who survive all the trials?

I raise my hand and ask Helen as much.

Her mouth tightens and her eyes narrow. 'They're criminals, Adelaide. Too old to be given a second chance. At this point, they have no chance at redemption. They would have already done it themselves if they thought they were capable. They'll still be executed should they survive all sixteen of the designed trials.'

My stomach drops. I already knew the answer. They don't care about these people. Not really. This is just another way to show who is in control. And even though they're preparing us to one day take their places, we'll never have any control.

I slump back into my seat and stop listening. Helen leaves the room and Professor Adcock is rambling on about how good a job we've done and all that pointless shit—I just cannot listen anymore. I may have to be here, but I don't have to participate. I don't have to be mentally present.

Isaac's hand stays gripped in mine, and I make a decision. It's time to tell him about the rebellion. And I think it's time we join.

The car drops us off outside our flat tower. Isaac starts to walk into the building, but I grab his hand.

'Can we take a walk?' I ask.

He smiles but it doesn't reach his eyes. 'Sure.'

Our fingers interlock and we walk towards the woods close to our flats. The woods Charmaine took me to all those months ago when she told me James was still alive. When they asked me to join the rebellion. *Children of the Realm.* That's what they call themselves. None of us were born under The Realm of Great Britain, back then it included Northern Ireland, and we had democracy. I guess we're all their Children now they've taken control of us.

I take off my backpack and tell Isaac to do the same, placing them behind a few trees and walk the next two hundred yards to the bench. The same bench. Before we sit, I take his face in my hands and kiss him, softly at first and then deeper, harder. He wraps his arms around me, pulling me against him and I run my hands through his hair. A shiver runs down my spine and all thoughts leave my mind. Why are we here again?

Isaac smiles against my lips, like he can hear my thoughts and breaks off the kiss. 'As great as this is, I don't think it's why you brought me here.'

I sigh and pull away. I sit on the bench and look up at the canopy of branches above us. The leaves are browning and falling so we can see the fading blue sky through the gaps. The days have started getting shorter. We'll leave in the morning in the dark and come home in the dark. Once again, our lives will be filled with gloom. As if it isn't already.

Isaac sits next to me and turns, pulling his left foot onto his right knee. And he waits. Waits for me to compose myself enough to tell him what I need to.

I look him in the eyes and see nothing but love. *Love*. A word we haven't said to each other yet. One I'm ready for, but not at the same time. Not if what I'm about to say will change things.

I sigh heavily and look into the trees around me. 'After the trials, Charmaine brought me here. It's where I first found out James is still alive.' Isaac frowns but lets me continue. 'I've barely seen him since, haven't wanted to see him. If it wasn't for what Charmaine told me, what she asked of me, I'd happily forget he even existed.'

Isaac plants both feet on the floor and leans his forearms against his thighs. 'What did she ask of you?'

'First, I need to tell you what they're part of.' He raises his eyebrows. 'They call themselves Children of the Realm. They're a rebel faction, working to undermine the government and eventually overthrow them.'

'And you're part of this?'

I shake my head. 'Charmaine asked me to join. But I didn't. Not then and not since. That's what all our fights have been about. Why I couldn't tell you and why I couldn't talk to her about it. She's my best friend but I felt like she just wanted to use me, you know?'

He nods. 'So now what?'

I clench my teeth and look away from him. 'What Helen announced today, what we're being forced to do it. It's too much, too far. I could handle my life being laid out in front of me, my choices taken away, as long as I had a little bit of freedom, but not this. I can't accept having a hand in killing people. I won't let them break me like that.'

He takes a deep breath and shifts his weight so he's leaning back against the bench. He scratches at his chin before saying, 'I agree.'

I look at him, my eyes widen. 'You do?'

He laughs a humourless laugh. 'Absolutely, I do. And I know what you're about to say and I want to join, too.'

My shoulders slump in relief. Of course he'd want to join, wouldn't ask any questions.

'But listen,' he says. 'If it gets too much, if they ask too much of us, we're out, okay?'

My eyebrows furrow. 'What do you mean?'

'I've seen reports of what some of these rebel groups do. Some of them attempt murder, Addy, and some of them get away with it.' I open my mouth to protest, reports can be faked, but he lifts his hand to stop me. 'I know, and I know they can be faked. But they'd show us these reports when I was working for the news station, and then we'd have to trickle in little bits of information. Not enough to let the public know how close the rebels ever got to the government.'

I chew the inside of my cheek. That makes sense. They wouldn't want anyone to get any ideas.

'You're right. If they ask too much of us, we're out.' I look him in the eyes. 'I'm so tired, Isaac.'

He pushes a loose strand of hair behind my ear and leans in close. 'I know, Addy. Me too.'

He kisses me softly. None of the heat from before but it's still as nice. We're in this together. Maybe I can tell him how I really feel now.

I start to speak but he gets there first. 'So, now what?'

'Now, we tell Charmaine.'

We walk back to the flat hand in hand, picking our bags up on the way. He comes into my flat behind me. I shout Charmaine and she comes out of her room. Alone. Ivy isn't here tonight then. Good. She yawns, probably waking up from her mid-afternoon nap. Although she only works part-time now at a London archiving factory, she tends to start around six a.m. She doesn't need to pay any bills, and I tell her I can easily give her half of my money. But she refuses to take it, saying she wants to earn it herself.

'Hey, Char,' I say.

'Hey. Good day at uni?'

'Not particularly.' She raises her eyebrows at me, then looks to Isaac who is watching the conversation with sombre eyes. 'Why don't we sit down.'

She narrows her eyes at me but sits on the corner of the sofa, and I sit next to Isaac.

'What's this about?' she asks, picking at a thread on the sleeve of her black hoodie.

'It's nothing to worry about,' I say, then chuckle. 'Well, that depends on who you're asking.'

She rolls her eyes. 'Get on with it then.'

'Right. Remember what you asked me after the trials in February? And what you've asked me since?'

She looks up into the corners of the room, at the cameras there watching us, and then back at me. 'Obviously,' she says.

'Well, it's time,' I say, and grab Isaac's hand. 'For both of us. We're in this together.'

She raises her eyebrows at me but doesn't comment. 'Great. About time.' She smiles, it reaches her eyes, and they shine at me. I can feel us becoming closer again with that one sentence. 'This'll be great, Addy, I promise. I'll let James know.'

She gets up off the sofa and goes into her room, taking a phone out of her pocket on the way.

I slump into the back of the sofa and look up at Isaac who is watching Charmaine with laughter in his eyes.

'What?' I ask.

He shakes his head with a grin. 'Was that just a flip phone she got out?'

I didn't get a close look at it, so I shrug. 'No idea.'

'I didn't even know they still existed. I've only seen them in museums. Relics now.' He chuckles. 'I'll let you get some rest, and see you in the morning?'

I smile and nod and lean in for a kiss. 'Goodnight, Isaac.'

A knock on the door startles me awake. I'm still on the sofa, still in the same position I was in when Isaac left. I get up and stretch. The person at the door knocks again.

'Alright, I'm coming!' I shout.

I open the door to find James stood there. Glowering at me.

He shoves past me into the flat and paces around the living room.

I roll my eyes. 'Come in then, I guess.'

He walks over to the window and without looking at me, finally speaks.

'Charmaine says you want us all to be friends,' he says. I suppose that's his term for joining the rebellion. 'Why now?'

I shrug. 'Does it matter? I just think we should all get along and that's all there is to it.'

'How do I know you're being sincere, and you're not working for *them*?' he asks, running a hand through his hair. Something I used to find so sexy, but now just annoys me.

'You don't. You'll just have to trust me.'

'I don't let just anyone become my friend, you know.'

I roll my eyes. '*You* were the one who wanted me, remember?'

He turns and faces me, crossing his arms. 'Yeah, in more ways than one,' he mutters.

I raise my eyebrows. Unbelievable. 'What was that?' I ask.

'Nothing. Fine then. You're in. We'll be the best of friends.'

I sigh, relieved I don't have to jump through any hoops. I need to get him to let Isaac join now. That's not going to be easy.

But first, 'I need to know why you made me think you were dead.'

He sighs and drops his arms. 'Does it matter?' he asks, repeating my own words back to me.

I clench my jaw. 'It matters to me.'

He stares at me for a long moment, his eyebrows furrowing as he tries to work me out. Finally, he relents.

'Okay,' he says. 'I needed to let you go, and it was the only way I knew how. It's that simple.'

'Are you serious? You could have just broken up with me. And what about your mum?'

His eyes darken and his mouth tightens. 'She has nothing to do with this.' He shakes his head. 'And anyway, who's to say you wouldn't have gone looking for me?'

I rub my eyebrows, a headache coming on. 'Do you think that little of me? I'd have let you go.'

'You didn't seem like you would at the time.'

I groan in frustration and throw my hands in the air. 'Right, because I was *so* needy, and you just couldn't be tied down.'

'Right.'

'Well, you didn't disappear, clearly. Only from my life. You're fine standing in my flat with the cameras on you. You're not scared of *them* seeing you.'

He shakes his head, looking away. 'They never needed to believe I was dead. I just needed to leave so I could continue with my plans.'

I grit my teeth. 'You could have told me.'

'You had your whole life ahead of you, I couldn't bring you into this at the time.'

'So did you.'

His face clouds in anger as he turns back to me. 'No. My mum had thrown me out, I didn't have a career, I didn't have uni like you did. I didn't have anyone or anything. I only had you. And that's not a life.'

'Yeah, and now you don't even have that.'

He walks over to me, towering above me and staring me down. 'Why don't you want me anymore?'

I take a step back. 'Are you serious?'

He nods. 'I know Isaac is in the picture now. But I thought we had something real, something worth fighting for. You don't forget a love like ours so easily. I'm sorry for leaving and lying to you, but I never stopped loving you.'

He grabs my face, forcing me to kiss him. For a moment, everything between us comes rushing back. Our first date in the pub, getting drunk and missing the last tram home. Our anniversaries, bowling and at the cinema, before the government took those small pleasures away from us. Trips to York, to the beach. Saying "I love you" for the first time. Meeting each other's parents.

And then all the bad. Him missing my birthday. Important events, family gatherings. The arguments, the sleepless nights wondering when he'd talk to me again. Every time he'd make me feel guilty for having any sort of emotion.

I push him away. 'Are you mad?' I demand, and he tries to walk towards me again. I put my hand up, stopping him, using my other hand to wipe my mouth. 'No. Stay the fuck away from me.'

'You still want me. I could feel it in that kiss.'

My nostrils flare, intense anger rising within me. 'Get fucked. I don't feel anything for you.'

'We were so good together; you have to remember.' He raises his hands in front of him, pleading with me. 'I would have done anything for you. You have to know that.'

He might as well have slapped me in the face.

Were we in the same relationship? All those nights counting to ten before responding to him calmly in case he decided I was being controlling, neurotic. All those tears, the nights spent drunk because that was the only way he could be with me. The mornings we'd wake up, hungover, and I could feel the love he had for me the night before fading away. All the lies, the arguments, the eventual hate. Am I really making it all up?

'You reminded me every. Single. Day. That I wasn't enough, and yet I still stayed. For you.' I poke his chest hard with my finger, making him stumble back slightly. 'Because I loved you so fucking much. It broke me every night knowing that I could never be enough, while I gave every part of myself to you,' I say through gritted teeth, anger rising in me as I say the words I was always too scared to voice when we were together. Before he disappeared. 'I waited for you to decide I was enough, but you never did. And then you died.' I roll my eyes at that. 'And my entire world fell apart. I grieved you for so long. But then I moved on. And I changed. I don't love you anymore.'

And I don't. I don't even hate him now. I just don't care.

He turns, growling in anger. 'You *are* enough.'

I smirk at him; I knew he'd say that. 'I know I am.' I shrug. 'But you're not.' A weight lifts from my chest, letting me breathe freely as

I finally come to this realisation. 'Now you need to get out. We can hang out another time. Charmaine and I will meet you wherever you want.'

'Addy—' he starts, but I don't let him finish.

I smirk again, 'Oh, and I'll be bringing Isaac.'

A look of shock takes over his face. 'Like hell you are.'

I just tilt my head at him, knowing I've won. 'It's me and him, or nothing.'

'Fine,' he says, storming out of the flat and slamming the door behind him.

CHAPTER TEN

I wake the next morning feeling like there's something sat on my chest. We've got a full week at uni before our first meeting with James, a full week of going through the trials that I want no part in.

I don't know if we're allowed to take sick days for uni, or if Helen will use that against us.

I turn over, pick up my phone from my bedside table and unplug it. I had the iPhone Elite for so many years, it's weird to have the most updated phone available now. It took some time to get used to it. It's so thin now, I don't know where they put the battery. And glass. I can see through it when I lock it. But it doesn't break when I drop it. The system is different too. Gone are many of the apps accessible ten years ago. The only social media app I have anymore is Facebook, and that's too limited to even bother using. But it works just like my old phone.

I scroll through the menu until I get to the preinstalled uni app to look at the Terms and Conditions. I chew on the inside of my cheek as I search for what I need. We're allowed one sick day a term, but any more than that will be investigated. As much as I want to crawl back under the covers and lay in the dark staring at the wall for hours, I don't think I can waste the day off just yet. Things will get worse for me; I can already feel the darkness pulling me in. I have to wait until I'm at my worst. But I fear it may be too late by then. Last night, after James left, Charmaine came out of her room to ask what all the shouting was about. After I told her, her face was red, and her eyes were bulging.

'He's such a bellend. I'll talk to him,' she'd said through gritted teeth. And that was that. No asking how I felt about it, the annoyance clear on my face. 'Your first meeting is Friday night, by the way. I'll take you both. You should tell Isaac what happened.'

And that's the first thing I'm going to do this morning. Before we leave to find out which *criminals* will be chosen for our practice trials. I grit my teeth. Unable to stop the bile rising in my throat. Executioners. That's what they are turning us into.

I take a breath, then another, gulping the air down. *My name is Adelaide Taylor, and I will not let them break me.*

Part of me is glad my parents aren't here today, to see what they're turning me into. To see the illusion of freedom I was given so smoothly ripped away. The curtain dropping, the participants of the trials lining up with me in the audience, a gun in my hand shooting each one in turn for no other reason than to entertain the government.

What would they think of me? Would they understand that I have no choice? In the grand scheme of things, I know all they'd want is for me to survive. I'm doing an okay job at that so far.

But what's the point in only surviving when there's no joy in life anymore?

A wave of calm washes over me. The rebellion. Children of the Realm. That's my choice, and it's getting easier by the second.

I get out of bed and have a quick shower, not wanting to be late so I can still talk to Isaac without prying ears around us. I dress in a black velvet dress with sheer sleeves. Maybe the only colour I'll wear from now on as I mourn my past self. I brush and dry my hair quickly, not bothering to style it. The cold air outside will ruin anything I do to it anyway.

I knock on Isaac's door, and he answers quickly, dressed in black, too.

He smirks as he looks me up and down. 'Same idea I guess,' he says and lets me into the flat.

I chew at my lip and sit on his sofa, crossing my legs beneath me. Shoes be damned. He raises an eyebrow but says nothing as he sits down.

'So, what I'm about to say is probably going to make you mad, but it's dealt with, and it won't happen again,' I say and his eyebrows furrow, but he doesn't speak. 'Last night, after you left, James came over and demanded answers about why I wanted to join his *club*. I didn't tell him anything, why we're joining isn't important.' I stop and take a deep breath, readying myself for what I'm about to say. 'And then he kissed me.'

Anger sparks in Isaac's eyes. 'He did what?' he asks through tight lips. The last time I saw him this angry was after the trials when I told him what Janesh did to us all. 'And what did you do?'

'I pushed him off me and told him to stay the fuck away from me,' I say through bated breath, hoping Isaac isn't about to show a jealous and insecure side and not believe me.

He releases a breath. Relief, disbelief, anger, I don't know. He shuffles next to me and puts a hand on my thigh. Gripping it, but not tightly, giving me a small smile.

'Thanks for telling me,' he says. 'He's a fucking prick and given the chance, I'd love to wipe that smirk off his face.' He releases a breath I didn't realise he was holding. 'But it sounds like you handled it well. You don't need me to fight your battles.'

I didn't notice I'd tensed up, but my shoulders relax, and I smile back at him. 'Damn right. But hey, if you feel the need to go all masculine on him, go right ahead,' I say. 'I'll always tell you these things, you know. Like you said a while ago, I don't want to be one of those couples that lies to each other and have unresolved issues because of it.'

'Same,' he says and lifts his hand to my face, stroking my cheek with his thumb. I lean into his touch as he presses forward and kisses my lips softly. He leans back, but only slightly, close enough that I could still kiss him, but he wants to say something. His breath shakes and his eyes lighten. 'I love you, Adelaide.'

My breath catches. What did he just say? His words repeat in my head in the few seconds I give myself. He loves me. *Me.* The broken shell of a person who is barely surviving in this world. A tear escapes my eye, and he frowns.

'If you don't—' he says but I put a finger against his lips, interrupting him.

'No, no, that's not it. I just can't believe you would love someone as fractured as me.'

His face relaxes. 'Addy, I'm broken too. And every broken part of my soul sees yours and sings, like our broken pieces fit together. We don't need to fix each other because we work. Together. Isn't that what we've always said?'

I nod and lean forward, kissing him softly. 'Isaac Webb, I love you too.'

The week passes with ease, each of the sixteen trials need to be built before testing them, so for now, we're just in lectures. Learning the history of what used to be the UK, and more about how the new government formed and why.

It's a skewed perspective, their version of history is different from ours. They're looking at it from a political point of view, which makes sense for a politics course I guess, but they're only exploring how it affected the upper-class citizens of the country.

Naturally, they'll show all the bad things though. Lots of riots from the poor, protests against what we all knew was coming. And the harsh punishments we received: tear gas, nights in prison, and worst of all, the executions. But they don't show the limits imposed on families. We could exchange money for vouchers to get a bundle of much needed essentials, but they'd barely last the week. The vouchers became too expensive, and the national minimum wage decreased. My mum and dad had savings, so we were okay until they died and then that was all taken from me.

No, they don't show the struggles we all faced just to get through each day, the crash in the housing market, the jobs disappearing, the arts being taken from us, so the only thing we had to get up for each day were the jobs the government decided the poor deserved, which barely paid enough to live on.

They talk about the introduction of the orphanages and why it happened. They couldn't trust young people to be unsupervised after the protests and riots. They thought it was our fault the country was becoming more liberal, and they couldn't have that. But they don't talk about the citizens who went into them. I want to give them a first-hand view of it, but Professor Adcock says it's not relevant and any opinions on the choice the government made regarding this are just that—opinions, and therefore not worthy of anyone's attention. So many people in our class take it all in as fact though, having grown up knowing nothing different. Their education paid for easily by their parents. They wouldn't know anything about real hard work.

I have to internally scold myself multiple times during the week whenever that thought comes into my head. It's not their fault they don't know any better. But they could choose to find out more.

Friday evening finally comes, and Isaac and I change out of our uni attire and put on jeans and jumpers with big coats. The air gets colder with each passing day, the closer we get to Christmas.

'We're walking,' Charmaine says. 'But it's not far, about thirty minutes. Leave your phones here.'

We both do as she says, putting them on the kitchen counter.

'Won't they find it weird that our phones say we're here when we'll be gone for longer than usual?' I ask.

Charmaine shakes her head. 'They don't check as much as they'd like you to believe. Besides, we're not going out the front door, so they won't even know we've left the building.'

I frown. 'Isn't that the only way out?'

Her eyes glisten with mischief. 'The only way for residents. There's a service exit with no cameras.'

'And you know this... how?'

She shrugs. 'I only work part-time now and there aren't meetings every day. I have too much free time and I get bored easily.'

I raise my eyebrows, but I don't say anything as we leave the flat and walk the opposite way down the corridor.

We come to a door that I've never seen before. Probably because I've never been down to this end of the hall. I shake my head. Isaac looks at me, questioning what's wrong, but I shake my head again and smile.

'Just having a conversation with myself in my head,' I say.

He smirks. 'Completely normal.'

I feign shock. 'Isaac Webb, how dare you imply it isn't?'

'I would never,' he says with a laugh and gives me a quick kiss.

Charmaine rolls her eyes. 'Come on,' she says and pushes open the door.

Strange that it isn't locked.

'No lift then?' I ask.

'Afraid not. It's only like twenty flights. You'll be getting your steps up.'

I groan. 'Yes, but I left my phone in the flat, so they won't even count.' I refuse to wear a watch that'll count them. Not after the one I had to wear during the trials. I don't wear anything on my wrists now, not even hair ties.

I follow her down the stairs—all twenty flights—and by the end, I'm out of breath. Apparently, my morning and evening runs don't help with stairs. I may have to adjust my exercises.

The crisp winter air hits my face, making it itch, and I wish I had moisturiser with me.

And we walk. Past the woods close to the flats, past all the old hotels that have been converted into flats. Past the long-closed tube stations, no longer needed as less and less people came into the city and the roads opened up for cars. Nobody could afford to keep using them anymore, so they just stopped. The trains were abandoned at stations as the drivers finished their shifts for the last time. Nobody ever thought to move them. I don't know what it's like down there, and I'm not sure I want to.

We walk past the London Eye, frozen in its final ride. Across what used to be called the Golden Jubilee bridge. It was renamed after the Prime Minister when the royal family were forced to abdicate and disappeared, most leaving the country before they were hunted down and executed in the name of democracy. It's called the John Anderson Bridge now. A tasteless name if you ask me.

There was a film I watched when I was younger, *28 Days Later,* I think it was called. When the film opens, there's just a man alone in London, nobody on the streets. The world is silent except for his footsteps. That's what it feels like walking to our meeting.

People still go out to restaurants in the evening. But the West End shut down a few years ago, nightclubs had no new music to play so they shut down. Cinemas couldn't afford to stay open. There's almost nothing to do. So, people stay home on a Friday night, enjoying the comforts of their homes.

Only the wealthy venture out. And even though I'm one of them, I don't know what any of them actually do for fun anymore.

I'm wealthy enough that my bank account has thousands sat in it untouched. Except the hundreds I take out in cash every now and then. £3,260 currently sits in bags behind the side of the bathtub. Waiting for me to do something. What that is though, I don't know yet.

So lost in my thoughts, I don't realise we've stopped. In front of what used to be Covent Garden. The sandstone building standing unused. Grass now grows in front of it, Clematis leaves reach up the side and over the top. The purple petals remind me too much of Wolfsbane and I shiver.

Signs of forgotten fashion brands hidden behind years of muck and disuse.

'Is this where the meeting is?' I ask.

'Yeah, down where the market used to be.'

I nod, remembering my childhood trips here. My mum would give me some spending money and I thought I was the richest person in the world buying replicas of Banksy art and studded belts. If only the girl I used to be could see me now.

We walk through the entrance, the sky above us hidden behind glass covered in dirt and plant life. Birds fly above us to nests above the shops in hidden alcoves. I can hear scuttling further inside the building and a shiver goes through me. I don't want to know what it is. We take the stairs down to the market—more stairs, I could really live without them—and towards the back, where a table is stood and a map is spread out.

James stands at the head of the table and smirks at me, raising his eyebrows when he looks at Isaac, who glimmers with anger. I roll my eyes and walk to the table, to the group of people standing around it. None of which I know.

A tall, dark haired girl with upturned eyes floats near James, touching his arm, his back, his neck every now and then.

'We're just waiting for two more members and then we can get started,' James announces.

Charmaine stands next to me and whispers the names of the people. 'The girl with James is Celie, his girlfriend. Not that it means anything to him.' She rolls her eyes. 'The man on his other side is Brendan, his right-hand man. The only person who knows as much as James, in case James is ever captured.' Brendan is tall and menacing, his dark eyes look us over, analysing us. 'Then there's Gareth, Alan, Lily, Charles, and Yu-Jun.' She points at each, a tall gangly ginger man, a bald black man, a small quiet girl who can't be older than eighteen, a sullen man who looks like he doesn't want to be here, and lastly, a Korean girl with sharp eyes. She leans back in her wheelchair, staring us down, but doesn't say anything.

Footsteps sound behind us.

'Ah, the last two members,' James says and gestures behind us. 'Addy, Isaac. I'm sure you know Ivy. And I'm definitely sure you know Janesh.'

CHAPTER ELEVEN

Ivy walks over to Charmaine and kisses her, once, twice, quickly. But Isaac and I just stare, eyes wide with shock, at Janesh. He was working for the government, how could they even want him to be part of the rebellion? What if he runs back to whoever his bosses were during the trials and tells them everything? How long has he even been here?

I know I'm ready to hear his side of the story, hear what made him do what he did to us. But this is too much, right? He shouldn't be in the depths of the rebellion.

I turn my back to him and he joins us at the table.

'I know you're wondering why Janesh is here,' James says and I nod. 'That's his story to tell, you'll hear it later.'

I cross my arms, annoyed that he wouldn't just fill us in, but I let it go. I'm here for me and Isaac, no one else.

'Right,' I say. 'So, now what?'

'Patience, my little recruit.'

I roll my eyes and let him proceed.

'Before we talk about anything in front of our new recruits, Addy, Isaac, and Ivy will go through initiation. Our own set of trials, if you will.' I can feel the blood rush from my face. 'Not the sort of trials you're thinking of. We won't be killing anyone. Well, not unless we have to.' He winks at Isaac.

What the fuck does that mean?

Isaac clenches his fist next to me, grinds his teeth. I know he's just as aware as I am of the threat James just made. Neither of us speak though as we wait for what is to come.

'You'll go through training. I know some of you exercise daily, running, weights, or whatever.' He flicks his wrist dismissively. 'And that's great. But we need more than that. You'll be trained in weapons and technology. You'll be taught how to not get caught. Which I'm sure you'll agree is the most important thing.' Everyone nods. 'You'll each get your own individual tests to make sure you're loyal to the cause.'

I came here hoping to escape the trials, and now it's like my entire life is filled with them. I loose a breath, my shoulders tightening with the stress about to be placed on them. I feel like I'll never get a moment's rest.

I'm so tired.

James resumes speaking, 'Tonight, the three of you will be spending the night in an abandoned tube station.' A shiver goes through me. Can he read my mind? Did he hear me thinking earlier that I never wanted to know what is down there? 'You'll be together with Janesh, who is your new group leader.' Isaac begins to protest and James gives him a sharp look, eyes narrowing. 'Yes, Isaac?'

Isaac stiffens at his tone. 'Why Janesh?'

'I won't tolerate hostility in this faction. Not now, not ever. If this is what pushes you to forgive Janesh and work with him, then so be it. He can tell you his story tonight. Is that okay with you?' he asks in a mocking tone.

Isaac rolls his eyes but nods.

'Great, glad you're on board,' James says through gritted teeth, clearly not happy I brought Isaac. 'I know it doesn't sound like a hard task, but wait until you're down there. You'll be going down to the Covent Garden tube station.' He looks down at mine and Isaac's Converse. I tilt my head, I don't know how I didn't realise he'd started wearing them, too. Somehow that makes him more attractive. 'I hope you're prepared for the walk, it won't be easy. Good luck in those shoes.' He winks at me and leaves.

Janesh motions to the right, where four bags have been laid out on the floor by the wall. 'Grab your bags guys, we need to leave now.'

'Did he have to choose a station that has a billion stairs?' I ask no one.

I'm sick of stairs after today. If I never have to use them again, it'll be too soon. My thighs burn from walking down the never-ending spiral. Isaac walks behind me, keeping pace but saying nothing, and Ivy behind him, with Janesh leading us. She's avoiding him. So much for having moved on.

There are no lights, but we've all been given torches and I shine mine at my feet, not wanting to trip and crash straight into a tiled wall.

A chill runs through the staircase, carried on a silent wind, which sends shivers down my arms despite the thick coat I'm wearing.

'Not much further now,' Janesh says over his shoulder.

'Says who,' I mutter but I'm ignored.

Finally, *finally,* I see an end to the stairs as the station widens before us. One hundred and ninety three steps I counted overall. And no step counter to make them worthwhile.

Janesh walks onto the platform, stopping in the middle and letting us join him. I look around with my torch. The white and yellow tiles of the station walls are covered in dirt and grime, the lack of cleaning in the last five years evident. Why they don't demolish the stations is beyond me. No train sits at this platform and the wind hisses through the tunnels. I walk to the edge of the platform. The tracks below me look clear and clean, which is weird. But I ignore them and look down towards the tunnels—an empty void of darkness. Nothing lives down here.

Janesh coughs and I turn my torch to him. He lifts his hand, covering his squinting eyes and I lower my torch a bit.

'Oops, sorry,' I say.

'It's fine,' Janesh says, looking away.

Ivy chews on her lips. 'So, now what?' she asks.

'Now, we have a choice. We can either stay out here or there's a room down the other end we can stay in. It's small, but big enough for four of us.'

Ivy tenses, the idea of close proximity with Janesh possibly too much for her to handle. Probably too much for all of us, to be fair. I cross my arms over my chest and keep quiet, letting the others decide.

Janesh sighs. 'Look, I know this isn't ideal but I've got a lot to tell you.' He looks around him and then back at the room at the end of the platform, his eyes brighten slightly with an idea. 'There's a rumour this platform is haunted.'

I roll my eyes. 'Shut up, you're just trying to get us into that room.'

He shrugs. 'Maybe. But do you want to risk it?'

A shiver goes through me but Isaac speaks before I can. 'Haunted by who?'

Ivy's eyes widen and she shakes her head. 'You don't honestly believe him, do you?'

'Why not?' Isaac asks, shrugging. 'It's London, there are hundreds of tales of hauntings. One of the only pages still active on Facebook is about ghost sightings, and London is the most popular.'

I chime in, 'Yeah, because this is where most of the population is now.'

'Sure,' he says, with a small smile and turns to Janesh. 'So, who is it haunted by?'

'William Terriss, he was murdered in the eighteen hundreds.'

I shake my head. 'Never heard of him.'

'So?' Janesh raises an eyebrow. 'Do you really want to chance it?'

Just as he finishes his sentence, a howl comes from the stairs behind us and I start walking towards the door.

'Yeah, fuck no,' I say. 'The room it is.'

The other three start walking behind me, hastening their steps as another howl comes from behind us again, closer this time. Another shiver goes through me and I'm taken back to the first night in the trials. We all laid in our tents silently as something growled and howled outside, killing Brett. That'll haunt me for the rest of my life.

I get to the door first and push down the handle, but it doesn't budge.

'Now what?' I ask, turning to the others.

Janesh takes a set of keys out of his pocket. 'These usually help,' he says.

I roll my eyes. 'Get on with it then.' He raises his eyebrows at me. 'Please,' I add.

What's wrong with me? For someone who said they want to hear his side of the story, I'm being awfully rude. I take a deep breath. It's just nerves. I don't want to be down here, let alone spend a night here.

Janesh opens the door and we all squeeze in behind him. It's basically the size of a box room in an old council house, but it'll do. Along one wall is a counter, but it's empty underneath. Against the wall opposite are towers of switched off controls. There's a slight hum in the air, like something, somewhere in the room is still plugged in, but I have no idea what.

'Might as well get comfortable,' Janesh says, taking a sleeping bag out of his backpack.

We all do the same, Isaac and I laying ours next to each other beneath the counter with Ivy at our feet and Janesh in the opposite corner.

We all sit on the floor and root through our bags, looking for food.

I find what I'm after. 'Who made us sandwiches?' I ask, taking the clingfilm off mine. Ham and butter. Good enough. 'They even used breadcakes. The superior sandwich bread.'

'I think you mean a morning roll,' Janesh says through a bite.

I draw my shoulders back. 'No, I mean a breadcake.'

'It's definitely a barm,' Isaac interjects.

'Pardon?' I blink at him, at his audacity. 'What is this foul language you speak?' I demand.

Ivy chuckles. 'Yeah, I've heard barm. Or cob.'

'This is madness. Aren't you both from the north? I can understand Janesh being wrong, but not you two.'

Isaac shrugs. 'Two against one. A barm it is.'

I finish my sandwich and cross my arms, leaning back. 'Whatever,' I say, declining to accept defeat and trying to move on. 'Now we've all finished eating, Janesh, do you want to tell us everything?'

'Everything,' he says bringing his knees up to his chest and wrapping his arms around them. 'Alright, I guess I'll go back to two years ago then.'

We all settle back to listen, nobody else speaking. I lean against Isaac, absorbing some of his warmth. He puts his arm around my shoulders, pulling me closer.

'Two years ago, my dad was the Chief Secretary to the government's treasury,' he starts, resting his chin on his arms. His eyes go distant, taking him away from this place. 'I say *was* because at the time, our family was in a bad way. My youngest sister, Nilan, was in and out of hospital constantly because of her lungs, and the medical bills started racking up. Even for someone working in the government, they were expensive. My dad wasn't paid nearly as much as you'd expect. They eventually found a tumour on her lungs and that sent the bills even higher. We stopped paying the mortgage in order to pay for her treatment. Anything left over was to feed the family. I was the only child of working age, but even with my job, we still didn't have enough.'

He pauses and takes a deep breath. 'And then suddenly, we did. My dad said he got a pay rise at work, they'd given everyone raises, he'd said.

But that wasn't true. My sister got better and then one day when we were all sitting down for tea, a group of security officials broke down our door and arrested my dad. He was stripped of his job and awaited execution. He'd been funneling funds from the treasury into his own account and it took months for anyone to notice because he was so trusted in his position. There aren't enough people in the government now to check these things constantly.'

He stops and looks at us all.

'I know what I'm about to say isn't fair, especially to those who wrongly lost their parents. But I didn't feel like I had a choice.' He glances at me, trying to catch my eye, but I won't look at him. I don't want to think of my parents right now. 'Anyway, one day the Prime Minister came to our house. It wasn't exactly a regular occurrence so we just assumed the worst. He explained he didn't want the public to know about this indiscretion as it would make them look weak. Like anyone could undermine them. They didn't need that.'

I chew the inside of my cheek. I've never even heard of his dad, let alone such a scandal. There were no changes to the government advertised over the last few years. Not since they took over and announced there wouldn't be any changes until the members of parliament either retired or died.

'The Prime Minister gave us a choice,' Janesh continues. His eyes are distant, like he's not really here. 'My dad could be executed quietly, or one of us could enter the trials and try to stop people from surviving. I know it was a bad choice, I know, but this is my dad. So I acccepted the proposition and my dad is in prison for twenty years. Who knows if we'll ever see him again.' He looks at Ivy. 'I never meant to kill anyone, I swear.'

She grits her teeth. 'Tell that to Violet.'

He sighs. 'I tried so hard not to actually hit someone, but I'm a shit shot. I don't expect you to forgive me, but I need you to understand why I did it.'

'Wait,' I say. 'You told me you hit her on purpose during the maze.'

He looks at the ground. 'I know, but I needed you to think the worst of me. I was trying to get in your head so you'd quit. I'm sorry.'

I take a deep breath as I think about what I need to say. He really did get in my head, and it's hard to forgive that. But if he's our group leader and we're going to be working together from now on, then we need to move on.

'Okay,' I say. 'So how did you join this rebellion? How did you find James?'

'James found me,' he says. 'He's got an inside man in the government, I don't know who. He knew what was going to happen and he asked me to work for him, too. I said yes because while I don't want them to execute my dad, I don't agree with anything they're doing. They're driving too many people into poverty and death. So here we are.'

'Here we are,' I agree. 'Alright. I'm not saying I forgive you, and I can't speak for Isaac or Ivy, but I get it. I would have probably done the same thing to save my parents.'

I see Isaac look at me from the corner of his eye, but he nods slowly. 'Same. So we move on.'

Ivy simmers. 'Easy for you two to say, he didn't kill someone you love.'

Janesh looks at his hands. 'I'll forever be sorry for that.'

'Sorry isn't good enough,' Ivy says. But she takes a deep breath, calming herself. 'But it'll have to be for now. I want to get back at *them* just as much as you do. So I agree. We move on. But we don't forget.'

She cuts Janesh a sharp look and his shoulders relax somewhat.

We're all quiet for a moment when the room starts to shake.

'What the hell is that?' I ask, panic rising in me.

Janesh stands, his eyes widening. 'I have no idea.' He leaves the room and we follow.

We get onto the platform just in time to see a train surge past us. It doesn't stop and we shrink back into darkness. We see people on a few of the carriages. Nobody looks out of the windows. It exits through the tunnel, leaving a gust of wind and dirt behind it.

'I thought the tubes weren't used anymore,' I say quietly. As if the people on the train can hear me.

'They're not,' Janesh says. I raise my eyebrows but he just shakes his head. 'I swear they're not and they haven't been for five years. That's what I was told. Some of the people in Children of the Realm have been staying down here every night and nobody has ever reported a train. I don't even know how it was running, there's no electricity down here anymore.'

I think back to when we arrived inside the room and step back in to listen again. 'I heard a hum before, just a spark of electricity. But it's gone. Maybe they just turn it on for the occasional train?'

Janesh frowns. 'But if that's true, then who's using them?'

'I don't know,' I say. 'But I bet James does. And I bet we were sent down here for a reason other than to just talk.'

Janesh's forehead wrinkles. 'What do you mean?'

I twist my mouth to the side, remembering exactly who my ex-boyfriend is. 'James always has some hidden plot. He'll never tell you the full truth. He wanted us down here. He wanted us to see that.'

'But why?'

I shake my head. 'I don't know, but we need to find out.'

Janesh sighs. 'We can't, not yet at least.'

The suffocating darkness comes crashing down and my shoulders tense. 'What do you mean?'

'James made sure the doors at the top of the stairs were locked once we got down here. We're stuck until morning.'

Chapter Twelve

We all clamber back into the room and sit on our sleeping bags defeated.

'I don't think I'll sleep now,' I say. My body feels like it's buzzing, any tiredness I gained from all the stairs has disappeared.

'Me neither,' Isaac says, holding his arm out for me to snuggle under.

Janesh sits across from us and leans his head against the wall. 'Sorry guys,' he says. 'I didn't know that would happen and James has my phone, so I can't even call him to ask if he knows anything about it.'

I sigh and pinch the bridge of my nose. 'It's fine, Janesh. He's unpredictable. Let's just hope he lets others in the faction know his plans, otherwise everyone is fucked.'

Janesh looks at me and nods. He gestures between me and Isaac with his hand. 'So, you managed to stay together after the trials then? How's that been?'

I look up at Isaac and he has a hint of humour in his eyes and he nods, encouraging me to tell the story. 'Honestly, it wasn't easy to begin with. You should have seen us on our first date.'

Janesh and Ivy both settle in, listening intently while I go on, my mind wandering back to that time.

When we came to our new homes after the trials, it took me two weeks to leave my bed. I had a lot of external injuries from the final trial, but I barely felt them with the pain of the grief eating away inside of me. I don't know how I managed to survive after Celeste died. I don't think I would have without Isaac pushing me on. But at that point, we were only speaking by text. My bed became my safe place as I let the darkness sink in and consume me. Charmaine would bring me meals but I'd barely eat, I couldn't after everything that had happened.

The pressure started to pull me under and I needed to get out, fill my lungs with some air that hadn't grown stale. I couldn't let myself become trapped like I'd been trapped in the trials, so I put on some exercise clothes, found some dance music—music that was approved by the government that is—and I went for a run. I shook away the darkness from my body, letting it become a shadow. I let a little bit of light back into my life.

I ran back into our building and knocked on Isaac's door. When he answered, his eyes widened and his mouth dropped. His eyes were rimmed red, probably mirroring mine, and he'd let his facial hair grow a bit. It suited him.

'You're out of bed,' he said.

I rolled my eyes and said, 'Clearly.'

'How are you doing?'

'Not great, but I'm ready to do better,' I said, and fluttered my eyelashes at him. 'So, about that date you promised.'

His face lit up in a smile. 'Finally,' he said and pulled me towards him, kissing me deeply before letting me go. 'I feel like I've been waiting forever to do that again.'

I smiled up at him. 'Me too,' I say. 'So, tonight?'

'Tonight. Where?'

I shrugged. 'You choose, I haven't been to London since I was a kid and I don't know what's open since I haven't left the flat in two weeks.'

He nodded. 'Great, wear something fancy,' he said with a wink and I left for my own flat.

When I got back into my room, I realised how much I hated it. The dull walls baring nothing of me and my memories, the white of the bedding, and I vowed to change it tomorrow. But I had a date that night, which meant getting myself ready.

I booked a last minute appointment at the hairdressers and got the cut I desperately needed, now I could afford to pay for someone to do it rather than doing it myself, and had my nails and eyebrows done. I even sprang for a leg wax, even though Isaac wouldn't see them yet. I wasn't ready to go further than kissing. It just helped me feel brand new.

I got home and found a lacy green dress, which almost made me spiral as I remembered wearing something similar in the trials. I decided then and there they wouldn't spoil everything for me and I put the dress on with some plain black tights and curled my hair. Charmaine had been shopping and bought me a lot of makeup, so I was spoiled for choice. Somehow, she'd remembered the one lipstick I had at the orphanage that I had nearly run out of and she got the exact same one. The red brought out the blue in my eyes and I was ready to go.

What I wasn't ready for was such a high-end restaurant. There were so many people in there, all used to that kind of place. The knives and forks clattered against plates. Waiters moved smoothly around the tables, invisible to everyone else. Couples around us talked loud enough for a chatter to echo through the room, but quiet enough that I couldn't hear any conversations. The energy was alive, but also incredibly suffocating. It took so much power to bring myself back to the moment, away from the anxiety threatening to send me straight back to my prison. But I did it, I brought myself back to Isaac.

I looked through the menu and I swear everything had mushrooms in it.

'Is everything okay?' Isaac asked as I grimaced at the seasoned pigeon breast on the menu.

'Have you eaten here before?' I asked trying to find even chips on the menu.

His forehead crumpled. 'No,' he said. 'I just thought something like this would be nice. I don't really know what food you like other than fish and potatoes.'

I raised my eyebrows. 'That sounds great'

His brows furrowed as he looked at the menu again. 'They have Chillean seabass with buttered new potatoes?'

I shook my head, a grin spreading on my face. 'No, fish and chips,' I said and could practically feel myself drooling.

He glanced at the menu. 'I don't think they have it. But maybe it's called something else. I don't think a place like this would serve chips.'

I stood and held my hand out. 'Let's get out of here.'

He chewed the inside of his cheek as he stared up at me. 'Are you sure?'

'Can you honestly tell me there's anything you would eat on that menu?'

He glanced at it again but stood up and entwined his fingers through mine. 'No, you're right, let's go. I'll just Google the closest chippy.'

A waiter walked past us as he said that, his mouth flung open and his hand flew to his chest like we'd said the most offensive thing imaginable. It made me laugh out loud. Definitely not the place to say things like that.

We left and had a great time together. I couldn't believe there was even a chippy still open, but I guess it's one of the only treats the working class still have.

Getting to know each other outside of the trials felt incredibly easy, it was like we hadn't spent any time apart.

After that, we couldn't keep away from each other. But we never went further than fumbling. Not until we were both ready, trying not to rush things like we did during the trials, not until after the beach trip, anyway.

I don't tell Janesh and Ivy about that first time, that's just between us.

'Anytime I feel like the darkness is going to come, I tell myself, "My name is Adelaide Taylor, and I will not let them break me,"' I say, finishing my story.

Ivy, legs crossed beneath her, leans her head back on the wall, and without looking at me asks, 'Does it work?'

I roll my shoulders back. 'Sometimes. Most of the time. But there are times when the depression wins and I just have to let it. Crawl under my covers again and just let myself be. Giving in helps, too. But that's for me. I won't break for them.'

Ivy nods slowly but doesn't say anything.

I let out a breath, tired of my own voice now. 'What about you?' I ask Janesh. 'What have the last nine months been like for you?'

He scowls. 'Not easy. I wish I could have the chance to date, but I haven't had time.'

It seems like such a simple thing, to have the chance to date now. Maybe that's the only small bit of freedom Isaac and I had achieved.

'Why?' I ask, genuinely curious about his answer. I want to know the depths of the things that have been taken from each of us.

'I'm paying back my dad's debts through my winnings. Instead of the ten thousand a month, I get a thousand and the rest goes straight back to the government. It's not enough for my family to live on, so between uni and these meetings, I've had to get a job as a political aid. My mum is back to working as a housekeeper, too, and some of my siblings have had to drop out of school and start working because we can't afford to pay for it anymore.'

'I'm surprised nobody knows about that,' I say quietly.

He shrugs. 'Can't make it look like a trial winner has a bad life after they promised us all second chances, can they?'

'I guess not,' I say, then look up at Ivy. 'What about you? What did you get up to before we all came to uni?'

She crosses her legs in front of her. 'Well, you know I only moved to London the week before uni?' I nod. 'Well, before that they gave us a five-bedroom house in Liverpool. It had a gym, and a hot tub, and everything. I didn't even know they had houses like that in Liverpool.'

Her eyes sparkle at the memory of such luxury.

'It was definitely better than the penthouse we have now,' she says. 'I feel like I can't breathe in London. We have no space. There, we had a huge garden at least.'

'So what did you do?'

'Not a lot,' she says with a sigh. 'I know I didn't know Violet for long, but you know full well how a situation like the one we were in could force relationships to progress quicker than normal.' Isaac and I nod. 'I spent a good few months mourning her and what could have been. I'd only go into the garden, because I didn't want to feel trapped. A lot like you, Addy.' She nods at me and I look at the floor. I don't want to feel connected about something so terrible. 'It took a while to get out of my depression, but I know if Violet had survived she wouldn't have sat around like that. She was stronger than me.'

Her shoulders droop, as if she's letting off some weight holding her back. 'So, I decided to be like her. I exercised daily, started going for walks around the neighbourhood. It gave me a good opportunity to listen to the gossip from the rich people around us. They all looked at me with pride in their eyes. Like it was their own accomplishment that they had a winner of the trials living in their neighbourhood and that I wasn't a criminal.' She shakes her head in disgust. 'But they didn't speak to me directly, except to ease their own guilt, to eagerly see how I was doing so they could pass it on to their friends. It's all fake in those neighbourhoods. I'm glad my building is empty now at least.'

I nod, completely understanding. Our block of flats isn't empty, but we rarely see our neighbours. Not even when we go down to the gym or leave for the day. It's like everyone knows we're coming and runs away before we get there. If they don't acknowledge us, they don't have to acknowledge what we went through. Lucky them.

We all fall into silence, letting ourselves settle into a relative peace. It's oddly nice to be around others who get it.

Isaac clears his throat. 'Addy pretty much told you everything, but that first two weeks were hell for me. I felt like I was stuck at the bottom of a pit and I couldn't get out. I didn't know anyone in the trials that well, other than Celeste I guess, but seeing so much death was too much.' His voices cracks as he speaks and he gives himself a moment before continuing. He looks down at me, a little bit of light in his eyes. 'Addy knocking on my door that day was a lifeline, she pulled me out from something I could have stayed in for the rest of my life. And at that moment, I decided I wouldn't let the past define me. I need to move past it. I won't forget everything, but I'll move on. If this uni course can help me become someone else, without losing who I am on the inside, I'll push through it.'

We all nod in agreement. I link my hand with his. We've had this conversation before in the darkness of our rooms. We can do this.

Nobody says anything for the rest of the night and we all fall asleep sat up.

The next morning, we all wake around the same time. No more trains came through the station. We trudge up the one hundred and ninety three stairs, my legs burning from all the walking the day before, and out into the fresh morning air. The white of the sky hurts my eyes and I have to cover them for a moment as I get used to it, before we start walking back into Covent Garden. There's a bite to the wind and it feels like snow might be coming just in time for Christmas.

Christmas. I haven't even thought about it before now. This is the first year in a long time I can actually celebrate it. It passed by so quickly while I was at the orphanage, the Madame never spoke of it.

I was always working that day anyway.

But not this year. This year is mine.

It'll be my first Christmas without my parents, too, if I don't include the last few. It feels like something presses on my chest and I can't breathe. I stop walking before we get inside and try to catch my breath.

It's such a stupid thing to worry about, but I don't even know where to buy a tree, let alone decorate one. My mum always did it, saying we'd just ruin her perfection if we touched it. I'm sure she wasn't wrong. I try to remember her lessons. Zigzag the lights up and down, baubles on next. Tinsel on last, if you want it, but some people think it's tacky. Not me. It'll always remind me of my childhood.

Isaac notices I've stopped walking and turns back. 'Everything okay?' he asks.

I nod. 'We need to go Christmas shopping.'

'Christmas. I didn't even realise we were that close to it.' He grimaces. 'I was going to go back home for it.'

I shrug. 'That makes sense.'

'You could come with me?' he says, hope in his voice.

I sigh. 'I'd love to, but I can't leave Charmaine. Not with it being the first year we can celebrate. And she'll be missing her parents, too, with no way to contact them.'

His eyes darken. 'I wish they'd open social media to other countries.'

'Me too. But they won't.' I clench my jaw, anger replacing my anxiety. 'Wouldn't want us to know how much better everyone else has it.'

'They could have it worse.' He frowns. 'But I guess we'll never know.' He interlocks our fingers and leans his forehead against mine. 'I want to stay with you. But my parents don't have anyone now with April gone, they're not ready for their first Christmas alone.'

'I get it. It's fine, Isaac. I promise. We can celebrate another day.'

He kisses me quickly, smiling against my lips. 'And I know just the way we can do that,' he says with a heated promise.

Something in me burns. 'I can't wait,' I say and give him a quick kiss. I sigh. 'Time to face James, I suppose.'

'I suppose so.'

We walk into the market, hand in hand, and find James and Janesh already in the middle of an argument.

'Was it a trap then?' Janesh demands.

James scowls. 'Of course not. I didn't know a train would go through that specific station.'

'But you knew they were running.'

Isaac and I look at each other before joining the fray.

'What's going on?' I ask.

Janesh rolls his eyes. 'James was just telling me how he knew trains had been running through the stations. He's known for weeks.'

James clenches his jaw, the tension on his face clear. 'And like I was explaining, I didn't know which stations they were going to.'

I frown, crossing my arms and standing straight. 'Do you know why they're running?'

'As far as I can gather, they're checking stations for people hiding. People like us. You got lucky this time. They clearly weren't looking for anyone at that station, otherwise they'd have stopped and got out.'

My eyes widen. 'What? And you didn't think that was something we needed to know?'

He shakes his head. 'You wouldn't have gone down there if I'd told you.' He smirks. 'Besides. Look at you all now. Teaming up on me. The best of friends. You can thank me later for that.'

I roll my eyes. 'But you didn't care if we'd get caught.'

He shrugs. 'You're the newest members of the faction. The most expendable.'

I clench my fist and move towards him, but Isaac puts a hand on my shoulder holding me back and I let him. 'This is bullshit.'

'Maybe,' James says with a smirk. 'But it's done, and now you know the risks of what we're doing. If you want out, now is your chance.'

'Fat chance of that,' Isaac says. 'If anything, it just makes us want to stay more. Right, Addy? Ivy?'

We both nod.

Ivy faces up to James. 'But don't think we'll forget this.'

James rolls his eyes. 'Whatever. Go home and shower, you all stink. Get some rest. You're back here tonight for training.'

He flicks his hand dismissively and turns his back to us.

Anger shakes through me but I keep my mouth shut. Now isn't the time, and he isn't the real source of my anger anyway.

We walk out. Ivy says she'll catch the bus home.

'I've got a car,' Janesh says. 'I could give you all a lift.'

Ivy shakes her head. 'I need to be alone for a bit. Decompress. I'll see you later?'

We nod and turn back to Janesh. 'I don't think I can walk the thirty minutes home,' I say, my legs screaming at me for rest. 'I'll accept the lift.'

Janesh relaxes his shoulders. A small friendship blooming between us once again. But it's on a thin string that could snap at any moment. I don't think I'll ever fully trust him. Not after how he betrayed us so easily in the trials. I just need to watch him.

CHAPTER THIRTEEN

I sleep longer than I thought I would, and it takes Charmaine banging on my door to make me wake up.

'I'm up,' I shout groggily.

'We're leaving in five minutes. Dress for exercise.'

I glance over at the clock. Just past five in the afternoon. My stomach grumbles, waking me more, and I force myself out of bed. After splashing cold water on my face to wake me up properly, I dress quickly in black exercise leggings, a stretchy t-shirt and trainers before slipping into my winter coat.

I dash into the kitchen and pick up an apple to eat on the way. No new messages on my phone means Isaac probably slept just as long as I did. I leave the phone on the counter and leave the flat with Charmaine, meeting Isaac in the hall.

'Morning?' he says with a lopsided smile.

'Something like that,' I reply through a bite of the apple.

It takes us just as long as last night to walk to Covent Garden, but at least we took the lift in the flats this time, so my legs aren't yet aching. Charmaine thinks it's fine to leave our phones every now and then, it's easy enough to forget them when we're not constantly using them these days.

The same group is stood around the table again, Ivy and Janesh beat us here, looking at a cluster of weapons. Guns. I grimace. How did they get them? Gun laws in this country were already strict enough before the new government took over. Practically nobody is allowed them now. The punishment is life in prison and a hefty fine, which most families can't afford.

'Great, you're just about on time,' James says looking up at us. 'The first part of your training starts today. Have you kept up with the running after the trials?' He looks at Isaac and I, then Ivy. We all nod. 'Good. You'll need to do that every morning and night. We need you fit enough to run at any given moment. Now, onto weapons.'

He looks down at all of them before choosing a small handgun and trying to hand it to me.

I put my hands up and back away. 'No way, I'm not touching that.'

He sighs. 'Still believe guns are the problem?'

I roll my eyes. A gun can easily be turned back on you, even with training. 'I'm just not comfortable using one. Why would I need to anyway?'

James looks at me sharply, his eyebrows furrowing in anger. 'I can't believe you even need to ask. This is the rebellion. We're at war with the government. You need protection.'

My shoulders drop. 'Fine, I need protection. Whatever. But does it have to be a gun?'

'What else would you suggest?'

I hate to think of it, after the trials I never wanted to see one again. But I feel more comfortable using one than a gun. 'A bow and arrow. I already know how to use that.'

He raises an eyebrow. 'Taking us back to the dark ages? No, not a chance. A gun is far easier to conceal. How would you explain being caught with a bow and arrow?' I don't have an answer for him, and he smirks. 'Exactly. So, you'll all be learning how to shoot. Do either of you have any problems with that?' He looks at Isaac and Ivy again.

Isaac looks down at me, his brow furrows in decision and I raise my own eyebrows, letting him know it's his decision. 'I-I've never used a gun before. But I'm willing to learn if it'll protect us.'

'Same,' Ivy says.

'Great,' James says, handing them each a handgun. 'Both of you go to the basement with Janesh, he'll show you the basics. Addy, you stay here. I need to give you your first test. You can join them after.'

'Just me?' I ask. 'Are the other two not being tested?'

He sighs. 'They are, but we don't have the time to tell you after training today. You'll all be doing some self-defence training tomorrow as well. Celie here will give you your instructions.'

The woman appears from the shadows behind him and gives me a dark smile. She leans up, her dark hair flowing flawlessly down her back, and gives him a quick kiss, before looking back at me.

'Follow me,' she says, tilting her head in the direction we need to walk.

I follow her up the stairs and into one of the old shops. I assume it was a clothing store, but it's empty except for some shelves, a counter at the back and some hangers spread sporadically on the floor. We go into a back room filled with ten screens, each showing a different section of Covent Garden, both inside and outside. Tall cupboards line the wall across from them.

Yu-Jun sits in front of the screens, monitoring them.

'Hey, could you leave us for ten minutes? I'll keep an eye on the screens,' Celie says.

Yu-Jun looks between us and smirks at Celie. 'Sure, have fun,' she says to me with a wink, before leaving the room, she has a few lights on her wheels that change colours with each spin.

'Is she security?' I ask.

Celie glowers at me. 'Of course not. We all take turns monitoring the cameras. I'm sure you'll have your chance. Now, sit.'

I raise my eyebrows at her, and she rolls her eyes, sitting in a leather computer chair. I sit in a metal foldaway chair next to her and cross my arms. She's got an attitude, and I'm pretty sure it's about James.

'We'll get started in a second,' she says, spinning her chair to face me. She leans forward, her forearms resting on her thighs, a scowl on her face. 'You need to stay away from James.'

I breathe out a laugh. 'Bit hard to do when we're all working together now, isn't it?'

Her scowl deepens, her green eyes flaring. 'He told me about your kiss, how you came onto him. He's mine, so back the fuck off.'

I roll my eyes. 'I didn't kiss him, he kissed me.'

She raises an eyebrow, a cocky look crossing her face. 'Sure, because everyone wants you, right? Lovable Adelaide, survivor of the trials. Well, I'm onto your little game, so you can stop now.'

Once again, I roll my eyes. I can tell there will be no getting through to her. It's clear I'm with Isaac and I feel nothing but disdain for

James, but I guess she can't see past whatever he's made her believe. 'Whatever,' I say. 'Can we move on?'

'Sure. Just let me know you understand first.' She smirks and sits back, crossing her arms.

'I understand.' That I don't want to be alone with James ever again, I don't add.

'Good. Now. Your first test.' She stands and moves to a cupboard, opening it and taking out a small, black, circular object and handing it to me. 'Do you know what that is?' She sits again.

I groan and look up at the ceiling. I really hope I don't have to work with this woman again, she's so frustrating. 'Why don't you just tell me?'

She chuckles. 'I could almost like you if I didn't despise you already.'

I raise an eyebrow and tap my foot impatiently. 'You don't even know me.'

'I know enough.' She kicks her feet onto the counter in front of her, crossing her right ankle over her left. 'That's a microphone. Click it and it'll turn on and start recording back to this computer. We'll be able to hear everything.'

I look at the object closely, trying to figure out where the microphone inside it is. But I give up, I don't need to know. I just need to know why I have it. 'So, what am I supposed to do with it?'

'I'm getting there. We know that Helen is an integral part of the next trials, and we know your group are planning the next round of them.' I raise my eyebrows and she laughs. 'Worried Charmaine told us? Well, don't. We have people everywhere. There's another one of our faction in your class. Hoity toity type. You'd never guess who. And that's the point.'

'Who—' I begin, but she holds up her hand, cutting me off.

'Right now, you only need to worry about you and your team. And of course, the people you've met this weekend. Anything more than that is classified until you pass your trials.' I stiffen and she gives me a smug look. 'Sorry, *tests*. Obviously, we wouldn't put you through anything like the trials. This week, you're going to arrange a meeting with Helen and plant this microphone in her office.'

'What would I meet her about?'

She waves her hand dismissively. 'I don't care, you can decide. Just don't be stupid about it.'

I roll my eyes. I'm sure I can come up with something. I really don't understand her problem with me.

'Is that everything then?'

'No,' she says and stands back up and collects a flip phone. 'This is yours for this week only. Let us know when you've planted the mic.' She hands me the phone. 'You can go now.'

She turns her back to me, watching nothing happening on the screens.

'Fine,' I say, and go back downstairs to the market. Behind the desk where we met up with everyone there are five big beanbags. Two people are sat on them: the young girl with strawberry blonde hair and shining blue eyes, next to her is the tall, redheaded man.

'Hey Adelaide, I'm Lily,' the girl says. 'Do you want to join us?'

I shrug. 'I guess. I need to join Isaac and Ivy though.' I look behind me to the door they went through for gun training. I can't hear anything, so the room must be soundproofed. I frown and look around. 'Where's Charmaine?'

'She's out on a mission,' Lily says with a wink and the man, Gareth, I think, laughs.

I take a seat on a purple beanbag and turn to Gareth. 'What's so funny?'

'Charmaine's mission. She was sent out for pizza.'

I frown. 'I thought she had more responsibility.'

'Oh, she does,' Gareth says. 'But it's going to be a slow few weeks while we get the three of you trained up for the proper missions.'

'Fair enough,' I say, realising they're putting a lot on hold just for three newcomers. My throat grows thick with the guilt. How much could they get done if we weren't here? I cough, clearing my throat. 'How long have you both been with James?'

They share a look before shrugging. 'She's here now, we might as well get to know her.'

I frown. 'What does that mean?'

'James has said a few things about you, about your fragility and how we shouldn't get too close to you.'

I laugh. Unbelievable. 'Well, if I'm so fragile, then why am I here?'

'That's what I mean,' Lily says, smiling weakly. 'Clearly, you're not. And you survived Celie, she can be a real bitch when she wants to be.'

'Ain't that the truth,' Gareth adds, chuckling.

Lily continues, 'So, to answer your question, I've only been here a few months. I heard rumours of royalists being in this group, I never agreed with what happened to them, so I wanted to join because of that.'

'Royalists?'

'Yeah, people who want to reinstate the royal family. These days they want an absolute monarchy to replace the government. I have to think that would be better.'

A shiver runs through me. Would a king or queen be better? I'm not sure.

My mind takes me back to one night when my parents were still alive.

It was late, about four years ago. I had an exam the next day, so I was still awake studying and I had gone downstairs for a glass of water. I remember hearing my mum and dad talking quietly in the living room, which was weird. I was in the attic room so I wouldn't have been able to hear them. The door to the room was ajar, so I stood in the hall, listening.

'What about the last royals?' my dad asked.

'Nobody knows about them, about her,' my mum responded. 'You know that.'

'But how can we be sure?'

'We just have to be, okay?' I'd never heard my mum sound so stern.

I stepped forward, and a floorboard creaked under my foot.

My parents were silent for a moment.

'Adelaide?' my mum said, louder than she'd been speaking previously. 'Is that you?'

I pushed open the door. 'Sorry,' I said. 'Just need a drink.'

'Of course, love, we're going to bed soon anyway.'

I nodded and went into the kitchen.

'Elaine,' I heard my dad whisper. Their hearing was starting to get worse, so they were always a bit louder than they thought they were.

'No, Jack, we can't talk about it now. Save it for later.'

I went back to studying for my exam and forgot about the conversation, it wasn't important to me.

I never asked about what I'd heard. Maybe I should have.

I push the thought away, not wanting to think about my parents now.

I nod at Gareth. 'What about you?'

'I joined a few years ago,' he says. 'James found me actually, I was trying to find us food from somewhere, I'd run out of money and vouchers, and we had nothing left to survive. James found me when I'd given up and was taking it out on a bus stop.' He chuckles darkly. 'We've been okay ever since.'

'We?' I ask, looking between them.

Lily nods. 'We're cousins. I wanted to join when Gareth did a few years ago, but James won't let children in.' She rolls her eyes. 'Why call your faction Children of the Realm if you're all adults?'

I chuckle. 'I did wonder. But nobody here even looks older than thirty.'

'Twenty-five,' Gareth corrects. 'James is running it like the laws for under twenty-fives.'

'That seems a bit like discrimination.'

He shrugs. 'There are plenty of other factions.'

I nod slowly. 'Ones that often get caught,' I say more to myself than them. 'And now they've introduced the trials, if anyone from here is caught, they could be sent to compete in them.'

Lily and Gareth share a dark look. Lily sighs. 'The whole point is to not get caught, though. And if we are sent to the trials, at least we have a few people who know what we're in for, right?'

She looks at me hopefully and my throat bobs. 'Right,' I say. 'I'll do whatever I can to help.'

'That's great to hear,' James says from behind me. 'Because you'll be telling us about each trial when you start running through them.'

I sigh. 'Naturally,' I say under my breath. I turn to look at him. 'What if they change them before they go live?'

He shrugs. 'Better to be slightly prepared than not at all.' The door behind him opens and shuts. 'Sounds like lunch is here.'

I'm standing underground in a makeshift gun range. It's not a huge room. There are round targets at one end, about the length of a tennis court away from me. The floor and walls are made out of grey steel, but James assures me the room is soundproof. Along the wall on my left is a cage filled with dozens of guns. A semi-automatic pistol gripped with both hands, and I can't breathe.

'Power,' James says from behind me. 'That's what you hold in your hands. Do you feel it?'

My hands are sweating and a bead of damp slides down my back. My mouth moistens and my jaw aches. I can feel myself needing to be sick, but I won't do that. I can't make myself look weak. Not here, not in front of James. I need to feel what he's telling me to feel.

I close my eyes and force myself to take deep breaths, willing the sickness away.

'I told you she doesn't have what it takes,' another voice from behind me says.

I open my eyes, dropping my hands to the sides, the gun gripped tightly in my right palm.

Brendan stands next to James. They're almost the same height, and they look similar with their dark hair and eyes. James hasn't given himself a buzz cut though. Brendan is bulkier too. I bet he spends all his free time in the gym. He stands with his arms crossed and an annoying smirk on his face.

I tilt my head, narrow my eyes and smile. 'Say that again.'

He raises an eyebrow, his smirk deepening. 'I said you don't have what it takes. You shouldn't be here. You're weak.'

Keeping the smile on my face, I walk towards him. 'Seems to me, the only weak one here is you.'

'Oh right, and why's that?'

I flutter my eyelashes. 'Who's holding the gun, you or me?'

He chuckles. 'Darling, you don't even know how to use it.'

My smile drops, and I lift the gun, inspecting it. Remembering what James told me, I hold the slide and punch the gun forward. I look inside the ejection port for the chamber, seeing the bullet loaded.

I lower the gun, and shrug. 'I survived the trials. Seems like it's easy enough.'

Brendan rolls his eyes. 'Go on then, darling, if you think you're good enough. Hit the middle of the target.'

I scowl. 'Don't call me darling.'

I turn my back to him before he can respond and walk up to the line at the end of the range.

I lift the gun, my finger along the slide as I take aim.

Trying to keep myself from shaking, I take a breath. It's just like shooting a bow and arrow. Except more powerful.

I brace my feet, centring myself. I close my left eye and focus on the bullseye. I'm not really sure why we're using these targets for practice, but thankfully, it's what I'm used to after the trials.

Lowering my finger to the trigger, I breathe in, and then as I breathe out, I press down.

The shot is the loudest thing I've ever heard, and it sends a tremble through my bones. I don't want to get used to this. But I fear I'll have to now.

Everything in my vision blurs as my breath quickens, and I fight to calm myself.

A slow clap starts from behind me and a hand lands on my shoulder, shocking me from my stupor. My hand is still on the gun, and I look down at it, then turn to look at who touched me.

James gives me a real smile, not his usual smirk. 'Not quite the centre, but good enough for your first try.'

'Great,' I say through quick breaths and slam the gun into his hands.

I walk out, tightening and untightening my hands so my nails keep digging in.

Laughter follows me out, but I don't turn to see who it is. I don't let them get a reaction out of me.

My name is Adelaide Taylor, and I will not let them break me.

CHaPTer Fourteen

The weekend passes quickly, the first self-defence class wears me out almost immediately. But at least I know how to throw a punch now. And I might run every day, but I don't use my other muscles much. I've tried weight training in the gym on the bottom floor of our block of flats, but I've never seen any appeal to it. The trainer says I'm going to have start doing it three times a week. I know Isaac does it that much, he's bulked out a lot in the last nine months. I might as well just join in. Besides, it might be fun watching him sweat.

I fell asleep in the bath last night, trying to massage the muscles as much as I could, but I barely made a dent in them. I felt like I couldn't breathe when I got out, the hot water too much after a day of so much exercise.

I really need a spa day.

When I get to uni, I go to the help desk and ask to make an appointment with Helen. They give me one at lunch time, and I'm told to go to her office. Perfect.

The morning seminar seems to go slowly. Bile rising in my throat occasionally. I'm nervous about what I have to do, and I can't seem to sit still. Isaac keeps hold of my hand the entire time, knowing what I'm doing, and my nails dig into his skin. I keep apologising, but he says he'd rather it be him than me. I chew the inside of my cheek so much that I draw blood. I can't stand this. I need the seminar to end, and I need to go. I don't even know if I'll be able to do it, and I feel like I could be sick.

Finally, the seminar ends. Isaac walks me to Helen's office and tells me he'll wait outside, then we can grab a small lunch. If I can eat by then. My stomach is in knots, and I don't think it'll accept anything any time soon. I give him a swift kiss and knock on the door.

'Come in,' Helen says from inside.

I raise my eyebrows at Isaac, *here goes*, I think.

Good luck, he mouths to me, and I nod. I can do this.

I enter the office.

'Ah, Adelaide, please take a seat,' Helen says. 'I was surprised to see this appointment added to my calendar. We have your one-to-one scheduled after we've tested the trials. I didn't expect to see you until then.' I nod. Me neither. 'Now, how can I help you?'

I pick at my nails beneath the desk, the mic burning a hole in my pocket.

'I'm struggling,' I say finally.

Helen raises her eyebrows at me. 'Go on.'

I take a deep breath, hoping the nerves I'm clearly showing make her believe what I'm about to say, rather than make her suspicious. 'It's just, I feel like I've got a lot of trauma from the trials. And now that I'm involved in the new trials, it's all coming back.' That's not a lie. 'I'm anxious all the time and I can feel depression setting in. It feels like it did after my parents were killed and I'm worried it'll get worse.'

Helen nods and gives me a sympathetic look, leaning her arms on the desk and clasping her hands together. 'I understand, Adelaide. It was a very difficult time. It was hard for me to watch; I can only imagine how it must have been to witness all that death for the first time.' She pauses and I nod. 'You must remember that you survived it, Adelaide! And the next trials will be filled with the worst kinds of criminals.' I grimace. 'I know, I know. You're still opposed to having a hand in their executions. But just think, you could also be helping some of them survive. You'll be giving them a second chance.'

'I hadn't thought of it like that,' I concede, and Helen looks satisfied. 'But I don't know if it completely helps. I still feel like my mental health is taking a toll.'

Helen leans back in her seat. 'Well, we can't have that, can we? Here's what I can offer. You obviously can't leave your class or course; you need to stay on track. You've been doing so well, I loved both of your group's ideas and I bet they will do well when it comes to voting. But if you really need help, then I can make you an appointment with one of the university counsellors. How about that?'

I breathe a sigh of relief, making her think I agree with her. 'That sounds like a great idea.'

She claps her hands together. 'Excellent,' she says. She grips her computer mouse, clicking a few times and turns her screen towards me. 'Which of these appointments this week would suit you best?'

I lean forwards, taking the mic out of my pocket and attaching it under the lip of the desk. I click it quickly to activate it and stand up to get a closer look at the screen.

'Thursday after class, I think.'

'That's booked for you then! I'll have a word with the counsellor before your first session, let her know about this conversation,' she says. 'Now, the new trials are completely confidential so you must only talk about your past, understand?'

I nod.

She smiles at me. 'Then you can go.'

'Thank you, Miss Hale,' I say and leave.

Isaac is leaning against the wall opposite the office.

'Well?' he asks.

I nod and his shoulders relax. 'I've got to do counselling on Thursday after uni now though.'

'Was it worth it?'

'I really hope so.'

In class that afternoon, we still haven't got anything to do, so Professor Adcock just tells us to get on with our morning assignments. I still don't really understand the ins and outs of introduction to politics, and I've never been good at essays, so I go through my book and find quotes I think will help support the point I've chosen to make for the first assignment: why the banning of guns in this country was a good thing. I smile to myself. The horrible training I had over the weekend at least gave me some perspective into why they're so bad. I started to feel the power they gave me, and it made me feel sick.

As we're packing up to leave the class, Professor Adcock asks us to be quiet.

'I know you're all getting restless waiting for us to start testing all of your trials, believe me I am, too,' he says, chuckling to himself. 'Tomorrow afternoon, we'll be taking a field trip.'

He pauses, letting the energy in the room grow in anticipation as people lean forward, waiting for the words to spill from his lips.

'That's right,' he says, looking smug at capturing the class's full attention. 'Tomorrow, we'll be visiting the Houses of Parliament.'

People sit back in their chairs, a few disappointed "ohs" rain through the class, but next to me, Isaac sucks in a sharp breath.

I lean over to him. 'What is it?' I whisper.

His jaw tightens. 'James knew. Somehow, he knew we'd be going tomorrow,' he whispers.

I chew at the bottom of my lip. 'What do you mean?'

'That's where my first test is.'

CHAPTER FIFTEEN

I texted James after I left Helen's office yesterday. I got a one-word reply: *good*. That's all. Then an hour later: *it works. Get rid of the phone on your way home.* So, we asked our driver to drop us closer to the Thames than our flat is, *we'll get tea out tonight*, we'd told him and sent him on his way. I took the battery and SIM card and threw each part into the Thames, one every five minutes. Hopefully they'll all float away into the sea, but at least if they just sink to the bottom, they'd all be found separately, I guess.

We had tea together then went back to Isaac's flat to get some alone time we'd been craving all weekend.

After lunch the next day, our entire class boards a coach to take us into the centre of London. They're a lot fancier than the coaches we had when I was at school. The seats are wider for one, and leather too. The coaches we used to have had scratchy material. There are charging points at each seat, and Wi-Fi. There are even screens behind the heads of every seat with Bluetooth for us to connect headphones if we wanted.

Isaac settles with his head back on the seat, eyes closed. He didn't sleep much last night, worried about what he has to do today. The rest of our class chatters around me, the trip riling them up as if they're kids. They all play with the screens in front of them, scrolling through the movies and TV channels.

I'm not bothered about any of it, so I spend the entire journey scrolling through Facebook. A habit from the past that I never really got over.

There's nothing worth reading anymore, not unless you want to read approved articles. I get enough of politics at uni—I don't need it in my free time.

Instagram is pretty much obsolete. There's no beauty in the world to capture anymore. Every now and then, someone will post a photo of food, but rather than a well-designed plate on a website, it'll often be a mother who had to use the last of her pay that month for a birthday meal and is proud of what they've put together. However small.

I've had a few of those meals myself.

But not anymore. Even still, I won't post photos of the indulgent meals I get to enjoy, it would just feel cruel.

I barely feel comfortable being labelled middle-class, I'm not going to shove that in people's faces.

Some of the women from my orphanage post on Facebook every now and then, subtle language to suggest how shit every day is under the Madame's control. I'd send them money if I could, but I tried the first month after the trials and they told me the Madame found out and demanded they give it all to her. So, it's not worth it. Not until they can move out at least.

We reach Westminster Bridge and all clamber out of the coach. We'll walk the rest of the way, but it's not like it's far. We're too close to Covent Garden though for my liking.

The sand-coloured limestone towers over us, Big Ben peaks out from behind. So much history lies within these walls. I don't know much about it, I never really watched the debates of the old governing parties that took place here, and nobody ever taught us the history of the place. The only thing I really know about is the Gunpowder Plot from the sixteen hundreds.

People are starting to forget about that now.

Bonfire night is no longer legally allowed to go ahead. Fireworks have been banned anyway, which was about the only enjoyable part of the night. I would have thought they'd want to continue celebrating a failed plot against the government. But I suppose the more people who know about it, the more it might give them ideas.

Professor Adcock steps in front of us. 'I know you're adults, but you're still under my supervision. Do not walk down the hallways in groups of more than two. Do not look anyone in the eye. And I'm sure I don't need to say it, but let's not fuck around, okay?'

A few of the other students chuckle but I can't, knowing what Isaac needs to do. He interlocks his fingers with my own, clasping tightly. It hurts a bit, but I don't tell him to stop. He's too nervous and he needs an anchor. These first tests seem more dangerous than they should be. The punishment unknown if we're caught. But we won't be. I silently promise Isaac this. He puts a pair of glasses on. There's a tiny camera in the corner of them, by the screw, that he needs for his test.

We walk through the entrance of the Houses of Parliament. The ceilings tower above us, arching at the top like in a cathedral. I stop to stare up at it. I haven't been in a building this decadent in years. My parents would have loved this place.

Isaac tugs my hand, reminding me not to get distracted and I start walking again. I look up at him guiltily, sorry for distracting him, but he just gives me a small smile of understanding.

We're taken to the House of Commons first, where they have all their big meetings. I don't know. My dad used to watch them when they were televised, but I was never much interested. I suppose I should have been. Maybe there were warnings about the direction of the country during the meetings, I don't know.

After that, we're taken into the Palace of Westminster. There are so many corridors and rooms, the tour guide doesn't take us into all of them. I feel like you could get lost here. Some of the rooms are numbered, and Isaac has to look for a specific one, but he won't tell me which. If he gets caught, he doesn't want me to know where he is, so I won't look for him. We had an argument about it this morning, but I finally conceded to his reasoning. I'm not happy about it though. I don't want to lose him.

We walk down a corridor and Isaac sucks in a sharp breath. I look up at him and he shakes his head. He won't say it out loud, but we just walked past the room. We don't stop though, continuing down the corridor and then the next with the group. We pass the toilets and turn around another corner.

Isaac gets the attention of the tour guide.

'Sorry, I just really need the toilet,' he says.

The tour guide sighs. 'Fine,' he says. 'I assume you saw them on the way past?' Isaac nods. 'Be quick. We'll continue down this hall and wait at the next corner.'

Isaac rushes back and I continue with the group. I look back every now and then, hoping he won't be long. I grind my teeth, counting the seconds. One-minute passes. Then two. At five minutes, the tour guide stops and points at me.

'You,' he says, and I raise my eyebrows, taken aback. 'Does he always take this long?'

I guess the tour guide noticed we were *together* together. But what a weird question to ask.

I shrug. 'I don't really keep track of his toilet habits.'

A few chuckles come from the class. I catch Janesh's eye. He's not laughing. He's chewing his bottom lip. Ivy is close to him, but if she knows about this task, she doesn't show it as she leans against the wall picking at her nails.

At that moment, Isaac comes running down the corridor slightly out of breath. He nods at me and apologises to the tour guide who just lets out a breath of exasperation. He tells the rest of the group no more stops until the end, which will be soon.

A bead of sweat drips down Isaac's temple and he grips my hand tightly. He won't look at me and I'm terrified something went wrong. But it can't be that bad if he's here, right?

At the end of the tour, the professor asks who will be getting back on the coach and we tell him we live close by, so we'll just walk home.

When we've walked far enough, I stop Isaac.

'What happened?' I ask.

He crouches and puts his hands over his head while he catches his breath. I wait, anxiety growing in my stomach, but I don't want to push him. The area isn't busy, and nobody walks past us, so there are no witnesses to his small breakdown.

I tell myself nothing is wrong; the alternative is too terrifying. I check around us. We're not being followed. But then again, we wouldn't need to be. They can track our phones. I'm thankful we've both shoved them to the bottom of our bags; in case they're recording our words.

He stands, takes a deep breath, and speaks quietly. 'I did it, I got the photo of the door, and all the individual locks for it. I don't know what James wants it for, but right now, I don't care.' He takes a deep breath and closes his eyes. 'Just as I took the last picture, someone came down the corridor and asked what the hell I was doing. He grabbed my arm and started to pull me away, telling me he was taking me to security. I told him I was on a tour with my uni group and Miss Helen Hale wouldn't be happy if I was left behind. Apparently, her name holds some sway there. He let me go and said to go ahead. But it was close.'

I lean my forehead against his. 'Too close,' I say. 'And I don't think that's going to be the closest we get to being caught either. James is really going to push us. He wants to know how much we can take.'

'I know, Addy,' he says. 'I'm about ready to run already, but I know you want to see this through. We tread carefully, though. We can't step out of line anywhere now.'

'Yeah, which sucks. I hate this fucking course. I'm no good at it.'

He chuckles. 'I don't think I'm any good at it either.'

I push at his shoulder. 'Hey, at least you have a journalism degree. You already did a politics module.'

'Nothing this intense, though.'

'I don't know what's worse. Being forced to make the trials or being thrown into these tests by James.' I take a step back. 'What's next, Isaac? What will he push us to do?'

'Who knows? As long as we don't have to kill anyone, I can just about live with it.'

I grimace. 'We're going to be surrounded by death for a long time with these trials.' I sigh. 'Come on, let's go home. We've got work to do.'

'No rest for the wicked.'

Something in my stomach plummets. 'Is that what we are?'

He gives me a half smile. 'Nah, we're the good guys.'

I hope he's right.

CHAPTer SIXTEEN

We're given no more tests for the rest of the week.

I have my first therapy session, which goes about as I expected. I can't talk about the things really bothering me, so I have to relive the trials. I was sick immediately after, I felt like I could have been back there, in the tent with Celeste. I don't know if I can take it every week.

Our training continues over the weekend. At the end of each night, we're barely awake enough to feed ourselves before we fall into bed.

On Monday morning, we hand in our essays and sit in our usual spots.

Professor Adcock walks to the front of the room, hands behind his back.

'Today is the first day we assess each of your trials. This morning, we'll be testing the train opening created by the afternoon class, this afternoon, the maze. Any questions before we leave?' Nobody says anything. 'Good, let's get going.'

Isaac and I look at each other but just shrug, there's no way of getting out of this now. At least we're together. Ivy and Janesh fall into step with us.

Ivy has dyed her hair again, an electric blue this time.

'I like your hair, Ivy,' I say. 'This might be your best colour yet.'

She gives me a short smile. 'Thanks, but I dunno. I liked the purple, too.'

'Well, you can always go back to it easily enough.'

It feels nice to talk about something as simple as hair for a change. There's nothing dangerous about it.

'I guess.' She chews on her bottom lip. 'Are you ready for this?'

I sigh. 'I don't think I'll ever be ready to see the trials again. But at least we're not in them.'

She crosses her arms tightly, almost hugging herself. 'I think I'd rather be in them than put someone else through them.'

I shrug. 'Either way, it's not going to be fun for us.'

We walk the rest of the way outside the uni building in silence. Parked outside is a coach. It's almost identical to the one we got on last week, but the windows are tinted.

Professor Adcock stands in front of us. 'I expect you to behave the same way you did at the Houses of Parliament. As you can see, the windows are blacked out,' he says. 'Unfortunately, you don't have permission to know the location of the trials. But you don't need it anyway, do you?' Not yet at least. 'Everyone on board, please.'

We all climb the few steps onto the coach, the inside is the same, it's just the windows that differ.

'Where do you think they are?' I ask as Isaac and I take our seats. I sit next to the window even though I can't look out. I just prefer to be away from people, I guess.

'Who knows? They can't be that far if we're doing two trials in one day. I bet they're close to where we did our exams and training.'

'And where was that?'

Isaac chuckles. 'I don't know everything, you know.'

'Are you sure? I feel like you're a fountain of knowledge. You know more than I do.'

He kisses the top of my forehead. 'That's not true.' He sighs. 'But I have been looking at boarding schools in the area, I know we were in or around London at the very least. Most of us got the train to St Pancras, right?' I nod. 'But there's nothing that looks remotely like the place we were staying. I'd think I was being a conspiracy theorist if it wasn't *this* government we were working with, but I swear they've wiped away any trace of where it is. Maybe we could take a trip to a library this weekend? They might have a record of it?'

'I don't know, I think if they were going to go to the trouble of eradicating it from the internet, they'd make sure there was no trace at all, even in the libraries.'

'You're probably right, worth a shot though.'

'Maybe, yeah. We can go if it'll make you feel better?' I look up at him and give him a small smile.

He nods. 'I think it would.'

'Then let's not wait until this weekend, let's go tonight.'

'Sounds good.'

We fall into a comfortable silence. I let my thoughts drift as we travel, the bumps in the road lulling me into a calmness. I think James will eventually want to know where everything is, so it's good that Isaac is looking into it. But at the same time, what if his Google searches are being monitored? They might find it strange he's looking up the location of our exams. It could be seen as natural curiosity, and he was a journalist before all of this, so researching things is almost instinctive to him. I can't help but worry. What we're doing with James and his faction is already dangerous enough, we don't need to be pushing even more.

But I can't take this away from him when it's clearly important. I really don't want to go back to the place where all our pain began, but I'd go anywhere with him if it'd help. We're all suffering from the traumas of our pasts, and dealing with it in our own ways, so I can't begrudge him that. I bet nothing will even come of this research anyway. It'll be fine. I'm sure it will.

I try to convince myself, and let it settle into the back of my mind, but there's still a gnawing feeling in my stomach that I can't quite ignore.

Before I can voice my concerns, the coach stops, and Professor Adcock stands up at the front and exits without a word.

We all follow him out and stand in a garage, not unlike the one we were in after our first trials. I suppose it's easier to reuse the buildings we were in than destroy them. But this first trial isn't even in a building. Unless they can completely disguise it so the criminals competing this morning think it's outside.

A door at the side of the garage opens and we walk into a room with cinema-style seats dotted around. The luxury ones that are slightly wider and recline. There's a screen at the front, which Helen stands before.

'Please, take a seat,' she says. Isaac, Ivy, Janesh, and I choose a row of four at the back. I need access to the exit if necessary. 'You might be wondering why you're in a cinema. Well. This is where the trial coordinators, me included, watch the trials, and monitor that everything is running smoothly. When the trials are active, there will be techs in here with laptops to control things in case anything goes wrong.' She looks over at me and then back around the room. 'I'm sure you all remember, in the last trials Angus tried to kill Adelaide. We do not allow the killing of other trial candidates, so he had to be eliminated. That would not have been possible without the people working out of this room, monitoring twenty-four-seven.'

I grimace at the memory. I still don't know what Janesh said to him to rile him up, but I doubt knowing would give me peace of mind anyway. There's every chance he would have been killed another way.

Helen continues, 'The group who designed this trial planned for it to be over the course of twenty-four hours. As we have sixteen trials to test, each will only be given four hours. You do not need to learn their names, or anything about them.' Of course, why humanise them? 'They have been instructed to keep their identities a secret, revealing them will count as failure and they will face consequences.'

I stiffen. These trials aren't designed to be kind. We weren't given the option to go easy on them, even for the opening trials. Four hours is brutal for what we planned. Although at least one part of ours will be easier, I guess. But if the coordinators have added extra consequences, I dread to think what is actually to come.

'Let the trials commence,' Helen says.

I shrink back in my seat and clasp Isaac's hand. He squeezes tightly, letting me know he's here if I need him.

The screen lights up, showing us the inside of the train carriage. It starts on one camera, then changes quickly to another, then another, before splitting the screen into eight so we've got the full picture of the carriage.

Twenty people sleep on bunks lined down both sides of the carriage, leaving the aisle empty. The only thing that lights up the room is the full moon outside and the clock counting down from five at one end of the carriage. The participants begin to wake up. It's a mix of men and women, the youngest must be about thirty. The oldest an eighty-year-old man, his hair thinning on his head. What must he have done to be here?

The train is moving slowly, creaking as it gains speed and shaking lightly, waking everyone up fully. They mutter between themselves, asking where they are. Nobody knows. They were given the option of execution, or the trials, and they all chose this, figuring they could still survive in the end. Each of them wears a grey jumpsuit, the same they wear in prison. A man of about forty steps off the lower bunk. As soon as both feet hit the floor, his body spasms. The front of his jumpsuit turns dark as he loses control of his bladder. Blood begins to leak from his nose and left ear, and he crumples to the floor. He spasms one last time before his body goes still. The timer stops. The floor opens beneath him, and his body is dumped on the track, and the timer restarts.

The first woman to wake up has hair cropped close to her head and her face is gaunt. 'Nobody step on the floor until the timer hits zero,' she says.

A few people murmur in agreement, some don't say anything.

Nobody moves, though. Finally, the countdown hits zero and goes dark. Still, nobody moves.

I chew the inside of my cheek; nothing will happen yet. I know that, and yet I still feel sick with anticipation. The trial coordinators could have added something to speed things up. I don't know.

The woman sighs and climbs down from the top bunk. She places one foot on the floor slowly, then the next. Nothing happens. She's safe. She breathes a sigh of relief and everyone else leaves their beds. The old man goes to the exit door. It opens with ease, showing fields moving past him. But he doesn't get to take in the view. Something from outside yanks him from his midsection. The top half of his body snaps backwards, folding down along his legs almost symmetrically. The two sections of his body fall to the ground. He's dead instantly. The body is sucked outside. The door slams shut.

We did this. Me and Isaac. Janesh and Ivy. We killed that man. And the man before. *I* did this.

'I can't watch this,' I say, standing up.

Helen notices me and comes over. 'Everything okay, Addy?' she asks.

'I just feel sick,' I say.

She nods. 'I understand. This is hard for everyone their first time. You can look away from the screen if you need to, but unfortunately, nobody can leave until break.'

Bile rises in my throat as I realise we're trapped here. Forced to watch what we have planned.

I don't sit. Has she forgotten how I got here?

'This isn't my first time,' I say.

Helen gives me a look of concern. 'I'm sorry, Adelaide, but the rules apply to everyone. We can't give you special treatment just because you're a trial winner.'

I just stare at her. She crosses her arms, not backing down. I won't win this one, so I take my seat. She gives me a smug smile and returns to her seat.

On the screen, a conductor enters the carriage.

'This journey lasts four hours,' he says. 'You will not be given food, but three bottles of water have been provided with cups at the back. If you survive the four hours, you will move onto the next trial tomorrow.'

He leaves again.

'Does anyone trust that water?' the woman says.

'Can't be any worse than the shit they give us in prison,' a man in his fifties says. He walks to the back where three two-litre bottles stand, and he pours himself a cup from the middle one. He sniffs it. 'Smells normal.'

He takes a sip. Nothing happens. That must be the clean water.

He finishes his cup and goes back to sit on his bunk.

Another person stands, a woman about the same age as the man. She walks and picks up the bottle on the right and pours a cup. With a shrug, she takes a sip. Nothing happens, so again, she walks back to her bunk. Then another man takes a sip from the same bottle. Just as he swallows, the woman who drank before him begins choking, her face going red, then purple. Her tongue swells, forcing her mouth open, and she can't swallow a breath.

I close my eyes. I already know what will happen next. I hear her body drop through a hatch, and the man who drank after her begins choking.

Four dead in the space of ten minutes.

Three people take a drink from the bottle on the left and are sent to the back of the train as they each begin vomiting the lack of contents in their stomachs. They're not dead yet, but with only two litres of clean water between sixteen of them, it doesn't look good.

And with what's to come, they need to stay hydrated.

CHAPTER SEVENTEEN

An hour passes with nothing happening. The criminals start to relax and talk about why they're there, without revealing too much about who they are. Some are murderers, some say they just had the misfortune of being in the wrong place at the wrong time. When rebel factions had a demonstration, they got caught up in it. They didn't join, but they didn't move either, believing they were right. Some of them actually *are* part of rebel factions.

'I honestly didn't know what I was getting myself into,' says the gaunt woman. 'If I could do it all over again, I don't know if I would. I don't know if prison could ever be worth that.'

A few others nod.

A bald man in his sixties speaks up. 'Prison isn't like it used to be. I was in thirty years ago for selling weed. We actually got three meals a day and—'

The sound cuts out as they continue their conversation. We're not allowed to know what the prisons are actually like. But if the volunteers thought this was a good option, they can't believe we'd think prison was a humane place to be.

The clock hits two hours and they must have gone silent because we can hear the rickety chugging of the train again. The students in the room are starting to get antsy waiting for the next horrible thing we decided to put in the trial. They start chatting amongst themselves. Some stand and stretch. Nobody is allowed to leave, even for the toilet. They don't know that they don't have to wait long though.

'What's that?' the gaunt woman says, looking at a dark mass growing in one corner.

The room we're in grows silent again.

Another woman, also skinny but with long brown hair, squints her eyes, trying to figure it out. I realise they're all malnourished. I'm not sure why that surprises me, but it does. It's a clear abuse of their human rights.

'I don't know, but it's getting closer. Hey,' the woman shouts to one of the sick people laid on the floor beneath the black mass. He doesn't move.

She starts to move towards him, to try to get him up and awake, but a string from the mass breaks off before she gets there. The train moves into the direct light of the fake full moon, illuminating the six spiders, their bodies about eight inches wide—not including their legs. The woman stumbles back, tripping over her feet and landing on the floor. The spiders reach the man laid on the floor and he starts screaming as they attack him with their venom. He stills, his body swelling beneath the bites and the spiders move on to search for more prey. They're climbing along the carriage walls and ceiling, six on the floor moving to the woman who tripped.

She grabs hold of the bunk bed and tries to climb on, only to see six spiders staring directly at her. One jumps from the ceiling and bites her in the neck before she has the chance to swipe it away.

She begins coughing. 'My mouth,' she says. 'It's too dry, I need water.'

She runs to the back, picking up the bottle in the middle again, downing a gulp straight from the mouth of it.

'That might be the best thing I've ever tasted,' she says. 'I could feel my body draining but as soon as I drank, it all disappeared.'

She doesn't know, but there's a cure in that water. It's the only thing that will help them now.

'That's great,' says the first woman, her eyes wide with terror as she backs towards the end of the carriage with the rest of the participants. 'Make sure you save some for everyone.'

The other woman nods. The two other people who drank the water that made them sick are attacked as easy prey. Luckily for them, it's over quickly. But it almost seems to bore the spiders as they start moving quicker to the herd of people.

'Weapons,' a tall bald man at the back says. 'We need weapons.'

The woman rolls her eyes. 'Where are we going to get those?'

'I don't know! I don't know.'

The woman who got bit breathes calmly. 'The bed,' she says. 'Look, the legs joining the bunks just slot in.'

She moves to the bed closest to her and lifts the top bunk with ease, removing the front two legs and letting the rest drop down. The mattress crashes to the floor, crushing the spiders closest to them.

The participants look at each other and nod as they quickly disassemble the beds and let the mattress fall on the remaining floor spiders.

One by one, the spiders land on each of them. Once they've all been bitten at least once, the spiders retreat to the other end of the carriage.

The participants scramble for the water as their mouths begin to dry and they lose energy. Their organs will begin to shut down if they don't get to it quick enough.

The bald man picks up the water on the left. 'I know it made the others sick, but it's still hydration, right? I'm sure I can stop myself being sick.'

With a shrug, he lifts the bottle to his lips.

'I wouldn't do that if I were you,' a man taking a sip of the clear water says, too late. 'Your body won't be able to take it.'

'Whatever,' the bald man says and takes a drink.

He puts it back on the shelf and a short woman with green hair picks up the bottle and follows suit. The man who advised them not to do it rolls his eyes. The rest of them have now had their fill of water and there's nothing left in the bottle.

They all sit, leaning against the walls, watching the two who drank the poisoned bottles.

It overcomes the woman first. She turns around and vomits. It seems to speed up the effects of the spider bite and she clutches at her throat as it closes up, suffocating her. Her face turns red, then an odd shade of purple, and she drops to the floor, which opens immediately and drops her to the tracks. I didn't even think to look at the other dead contestants to see if this happened, but I assume it couldn't while there were spiders everywhere. My question is answered when I look to one of the other cameras and watch them drop below.

The bald man is holding his face, turning red as he tries to stop himself being sick. He bends over as his stomach convulses and water begins to dribble out the sides of his mouth. He slaps a hand over it, trying to stop and swallow it, but he can't. He eventually lets it go and is dropped out of the train before he can even be pronounced dead.

That leaves eleven. They watch the spiders watch them back in silence. Nobody moves, I guess they think if they do, they might trigger something worse.

The screen goes dark. Somehow, the four hours have passed. Eleven survived to move on to tomorrow's trial.

I'm sick on our lunch break, keeping nothing down, like I've poisoned myself with the water I put there to kill the others. How can I be a part of this? Wouldn't it be better to lose everything now than continue with the execution of others? I want to leave, to get out. But if I go now, I won't be able to help the Children of the Realm.

I leave the bathroom and go into the cafeteria, choosing a sports drink over water and food. I don't think I can face either yet. Once everyone has finished eating, Helen comes into the room.

'Everyone, listen please,' she says. 'We'll be testing the second opening trial today. But after that, you're free to go. We'll have another fourteen to get through. We've decided to cut down the time for the rest to two hours where we're able, so we'll be done with them by the end of the week.'

I relax slightly. Only four and a half more days then.

We go back into the cinema room and watch another twenty so-called criminals enter their trial. Only nine of them survive the maze. I honestly don't know how any of them got through it. I won't be watching it when it airs, that's for sure. I can't go through that again.

It's put to a vote after we watched the second opening trial. A vote to pick which one will go ahead in January. Ours isn't chosen. And I'm thankful that we don't have to suffer the trauma of handing more people their deaths. I just hope our second trial isn't picked.

Isaac walks me to my door when we get home. I'm so tired. I wasn't even part of the trials, but I felt every death like it was me.

Isaac gives me a weak smile, pain shining in his eyes. He brushes a piece of my hair behind my ear. 'Get some sleep, we'll do the library another day.'

I frown. 'Are you sure?' I ask, my voice barely coming out as more than a whisper. My throat too sore after being sick.

'Completely. It's not important. You taking care of yourself is what matters.'

I lean my head against his chest, and he wraps his arms around me. 'I knew it would be hard, but I just... it's impossible.' I feel him nod against me. 'Can you stay with me?'

'Of course,' he says.

I lead him into the flat. Charmaine isn't home yet thankfully. I don't have the strength to relay the day to her.

I let Isaac undress as I go into the bathroom and brush my teeth. I stare at myself in the mirror as I will the hole in my chest to close. I just want to stop feeling this pain.

They're fighting for a second chance; one they won't get when this all ends in execution anyway. But maybe just this small sense of hope is a good reprieve for them, something to hold onto because they don't know the ultimate outcome. Maybe this is a good thing.

I clench my teeth. No. I can't let myself think that way. As soon as I give in to that feeling, I become one of them. A cold, heartless person who doesn't value human life. I won't do it. *I won't let them break me.*

I take a deep breath, composing myself. I go back into my bedroom and get undressed.

'Can I sleep in your t-shirt?' I ask Isaac.

He gives me a small smile from my bed. 'I'd love that.'

I put it on, letting his scent overwhelm me. *This,* right here. This is something good, something I'm so afraid to lose. Isaac pulls back the covers and I crawl into bed, tucking my head into his chest, my arm across his body and my leg over both of his. He tucks the cover back across us, enclosing us in warmth.

His hand trails along my back, lulling me into a stillness I don't think I could get anywhere else.

I look up at him, stroke my hand along his jaw. 'I know we keep saying we'll get out if we have to,' I whisper. 'But I just need you to know that I have a plan. If we need to run, I've got a safety net for us.'

He kisses the top of my head. 'Of course you do,' he whispers, pulling me closer so I'm pressed against him. 'One of the things I love about you is how organised you are, you know?'

I smile up at him and draw him down for a kiss. 'I didn't know, but I'm glad to hear it.' I sigh. 'I really love you. More than I thought was possible.'

'I really love you too, Adelaide,' he says. I love it when he says my name rather than calling me Addy. His deep voice envelopes it like it's his favourite thing to say. 'We'll get through this, I promise. I'm not going to let the darkness take us.'

I love him even more for that. For knowing I can feel it at the edge of my mind without even having to tell him.

I lean up for another kiss, deepening it, and pressing myself fully against his body.

He groans against my mouth but pulls away, catching my wrist in his hand. 'As much as I love where this is going, you're exhausted. We both are. So how about we get some sleep and pick this up in the morning?'

'But—' I start to say, but my body betrays me with a yawn. Isaac gives me a triumphant smile. 'Fine, you're right.'

I lower my head back to his chest and he kisses the top of my head. 'Of course I'm right,' he says with a chuckle.

I let him win this one, my body already soothed enough to gently fall asleep.

The week passes horribly slowly as we witness so many deaths. Our second trial is chosen, which means we'll have to be here to watch it all over again. We barely speak to Ivy and Janesh during our breaks, all of us caught up in our own grief, unwilling to share it.

At the end of the week, we go to Covent Garden for a meeting, straight from uni. We turned our phones off when we left so they couldn't track us here.

James is having a hushed conversation with Lily, but I overhear the last part of it.

'Everything is set down there for tomorrow, yes?' he demands.

Lily nods. 'But James,' she says. 'What if one of the patrols comes?'

He rolls his eyes. 'Then you hide. Do not get caught.'

She looks at her shoes but nods. I walk closer to the table and cough, announcing our arrival. Lily's head snaps up, her eyes filling with the shadow of tears, but she wipes them away quickly, replacing them with a smile.

'Hey guys,' she says, cheerfully. 'Good week?'

I stiffen and let Isaac answer for me. 'If you call watching forty people die by our hand good, then sure.' Lily winces and he sighs. 'Sorry, we're all just a bit stressed out.'

She shrugs and looks at James quickly. 'I know the feeling,' she mutters. 'See you later. And good luck.'

She leaves the room. What did that mean?

Celie enters and stands next to James, possessively running a hand down his back. He shrugs her off and a look of hurt flashes across her face, quickly replaced by anger.

James looks up from his computer. 'So, the trials. Which of them did they pick?'

We relay all the information. There will be eight stages in total spotted around the horrorfest, and he wants the details for each one, and how all the deaths transpire, so it takes a while. We sit at the table as dinner arrives. Chinese tonight. I ordered prawn balls with curry sauce and egg fried rice, but I can barely taste it.

We finish our food as the conversation draws to a conclusion. James stands again, talking to us all. Ivy and Janesh arrived shortly after we did, filling in the specifics we missed.

'Ivy passed her final test this week,' James says. I raise my eyebrows. 'You don't need to know what it is. Adelaide and Isaac, you have one more test. I'll even let you do this one together.'

He smirks, like he's some big champion of our relationship. Being so kind.

'Get on with it then,' I say.

He scowls. I didn't give him the response he wanted. His cheek twitches as he fights against what he really wants to say.

'Right,' he continues. 'I need you to find out where the trial centre is.'

Chapter Eighteen

'No,' I say before I can stop myself.

James raises an eyebrow at me. 'No? You think you have a choice in the matter? If you want to stay, you'll do as I say.'

My throat closes up. 'Not that. I can't do that.'

He sighs. 'And why not?'

'This week *broke* me, James,' I say, my voice cracking. 'I can't delve further into the trials. I won't.'

Isaac puts a hand on my back, and I lean into his warmth. 'I agree, you're asking too much,' he says.

James scowls. 'Don't you think we're all doing too much? We're all constantly putting ourselves at risk. What makes you so special? Everyone here is pushing themselves to their limits. Are you so selfish that you think others should be doing these things for you while you sit back in your fancy homes watching everyone else sacrifice themselves completely to the cause?' He pauses, seemingly out of breath.

He clears his throat. 'If we want to take the government down, this is what we have to do, and this is what you're both doing. You have no say in this.'

'I can't,' I say.

James slams a hand on the table, making me jump. 'This isn't a debate,' he shouts. 'If you don't do this, you're out.' I start to answer, maybe that would be the best thing for us. 'Yes, I'm sure you'd love that. But you're in too deep now, I'm sure you'd get yourselves caught trying to run off together. Are the trials not enough to show you what they are? They are *monsters*. We need to stop them.'

I take a deep breath. We do. But I don't know if I'm ready for that yet.

'I think you both need more of a reminder. Celie,' he says, drawing her close to him. 'You're taking Addy on a field trip this weekend.'

A look of dismay crosses her face as her mouth drops. 'What? Why me?'

'Because I said so,' he snaps.

Celie glares at him, he glares right back. He wins, of course. He always does.

She rolls her eyes. 'Fine, whatever. Where are we going?'

'Hope Valley. You remember the place?' She nods. 'Good. Get some camping gear and sign out one of the cars. You need to go immediately.'

'What about me?' Isaac says.

James looks at me. 'I'll tell you when they're gone.'

I roll my eyes but turn away from him. He leaves the room with Celie; I assume to prepare whatever he's doing.

I grip my hand in Isaac's. 'He's baiting us,' I say. 'I don't know what for but splitting us up for the weekend is part of it.'

Isaac nods. 'I know, we can't rise to it.' He kisses me softly. 'Stay safe this weekend, okay? I don't completely trust Celie.'

'Me neither, not when she's so enamoured by James.'

Celie comes back into the room and tosses a bag at my feet.

'Come on,' she says. 'We need to go.'

She stalks out, but I don't follow immediately.

I crush my lips against Isaac's. 'I love you,' I say, breaking away. 'Be careful.'

'You too, I love you.'

His eyes flash with pain, this is the first time we'll have really been apart for months. I guess this is a test for us as well.

I pick up the backpack, leave the room, and go outside.

Celie has parked up a Suzuki Jimny Jeep outside the building. Old but practical, I guess. I climb in the car, chucking my bag in the back.

'Let's get this over with,' Celie says, starting the engine.

I look through the glove compartment and find some CDs, surprised to find that they have McFly. They were my favourite band growing up, *RadioActive* was my favourite album of all time. I went to see every concert of theirs until they disappeared.

I don't know what happened to them. They started to release more and more political music and the government didn't like that, so they banned them from the industry, along with so many others. But I still have my MP3 player with their music on.

'Do you care if I put this on?' I ask.

Celie shrugs but looks at the CD. Her eyebrows furrow. 'That's my CD,' she says, sounding surprised I picked it. 'Yeah, put it on.'

We don't speak during the journey, only stopping every so often to fill up on fuel and get some food. We avoid all the major cities and drive mainly through country roads. It's quieter out here, the only sound being the music in the car and the engine. We don't pass any other cars; the road is completely ours. I miss road trips like this. I mean, Celie isn't exactly the best companion, but at least she's not being a bitch.

The car slows as we come to an old train station. Night has fallen and there are no lights on. It probably isn't in use anymore. The car headlights shine on a sign—Bamford.

'What's here?' I ask.

'Nothing,' Celie says, stopping the car and shutting it off. 'We're walking from here.'

I groan inwardly. We're surrounded by hills; this isn't going to be fun.

'Do I take my phone or leave it here?'

Celie rolls her eyes. 'You know the answer to that.'

She's right, I guess. I'm not an idiot. It was already turned off, so they won't learn our location. Unless they can turn it back on somehow. I put it in the glove compartment.

I get out of the car and pull my seat forward, getting my bag and coat.

'Your gun is in there as well. I doubt you'll need it, but I'd rather we be prepared where we're going.'

'And where *are* we going?'

'Nowhere tonight. We're going to walk as quickly as possible and camp out of sight of this train station.'

'But it's not in use, is it?'

'Not by the general public, no. The general public typically don't come here anymore. There's a factory that we're going to tomorrow that security officials come to on business.'

'So why have we parked here?'

She shrugs. 'Every now and then campers still come out here. Not usually in December, but it's not unheard of. It's fine.'

She takes two torches out of her bag, handing me one.

'Come on, I think a train is due soon. You're too well known for them to think you're just a casual camper. Not here.'

'You're being awfully nice.'

She rolls her eyes. 'Don't think it changes anything. I don't want you dead, even if I don't like you. Besides, James would kill me if I let anything happen to his precious Adelaide.'

'I'm not his precious—you know what, nevermind,' I say. I don't think there's any getting through to her. I take a deep breath before I speak again. 'Alright then, lead the way.'

We take off, our torches lighting our way as we crest the first hill. My lungs burn and I'm getting a stitch. Even with all our training, I'm not really used to hills anymore. Sheffield was basically all hills. I had to walk up and down them every day to get to work and back. It was hard then, but not as hard as this.

We take a break at the top, both out of breath. Behind us, I hear the whistle of a train pulling into a station and look across at Celie.

'Come on,' she says. 'We just need to get over this hill and then we can set up camp in the valley at the bottom.'

I just nod. We're close to where my dad used to bring me camping. Castleton is part of Hope Valley. But I don't know my way around, especially not in the dark. I just have to trust Celie. And trust she meant she doesn't want me dead.

We walk quickly down the hill, almost too quickly for the wet grass. My feet slip multiple times but by some miracle, I manage to stay upright.

When we get to the bottom, Celie stops, and I realise she's holding a bag shaped like a tube.

'Hold the torch on me, would you?' she asks.

She pulls a dark green tent out and lays it flat on the ground, showing its octagon shape. She takes out the corner pegs, putting them in their holes and stomping them in the ground. The poles attach easily. I ask if she needs help, but she just says it'd slow her down having to tell me what to do and she's done this many times. She proves that with how quick she erects the tent.

Soon, we're laid inside, the tent closed to the wind outside. An LED lantern hangs above us, casting shadows in the corners. We brought some freeze-dried food with us and eat a quick meal of macaroni cheese.

We don't know what prowls these hills at night anymore. Not now there's much less human life. As far as I know, the little villages like Castleton and Hope are abandoned now. The people living there had to move into cities once public transport was limited. I suppose they could be used as easy hideouts for people like us, but at the same time, wouldn't they be searched frequently? I don't voice my questions, there's no use getting on Celie's nerves right now.

She isn't asleep yet, her breathing too quick for that. I turn onto my left to look at her. I hadn't noticed before just how pretty she actually is. Her emerald eyes turn up slightly on the corners, she has full, plump lips and a little button nose. Her long black hair is cut perfectly to suit her heart-shaped face. I can see why James likes her. Her jaw tenses.

'Why are you looking at me?' she asks.

I sigh. 'I don't know. Are you alright?'

She rolls her eyes. 'Why wouldn't I be?'

'Well, James sent you out here with someone you hate to do god knows what.'

'You know James, he likes to push people.'

'I do know that, yes. Very well.'

Her eyes flick to me. She observes me for a moment. 'Was it always bad?' she asks quietly.

'With James?' She nods. 'No, not always. It was actually great for a while.'

She turns onto her right side, resting her cheek on the crook of her arm, and looks at me properly, no hate in her eyes, only questions. 'How did you meet?' she asks.

I lose a breath. I haven't even told Isaac most of the story of me and James. It's never really mattered. 'It was six years ago,' I say. 'I'd just started uni, I wanted to be a vet back then. I still wouldn't mind it, to be honest, if I had that choice.' I tense and take a breath; this isn't about that. 'Someone I knew had an older brother in the area and he was having a house party. James was there, and we hit it off immediately, talking all night. We got exceedingly drunk, and I went back to his.'

Celie scowls. 'Hey, I didn't ask about you having sex.'

I shake my head. 'We didn't. I crashed on his sofa, he made me breakfast and then drove me home. And then we went on a date a week later: just to the pub where we got very drunk. It was weirdly nice.'

'Yeah,' Celie says. 'Nice. I wish it could be as simple as that these days.'

'What about you? How did you meet him?'

She chews on her lip, like she's trying to decide what to tell me. She breathes out. 'A year ago, I was homeless. My parents had been killed and no orphanage would take me in, I was too close to twenty-five and a waste of money.' I scrunch my nose in disgust. Are there no good orphanages in this country? 'Anyway, he found me. Offered me a better life and I took it. He really draws you in with those dark eyes and easy smile.'

I nod. 'Did you ever manage to go on any dates or anything, or did you just end up together?'

'Sort of both. We were working together late one night, and he kissed me. He told me I was special, and he felt like he couldn't trust anyone but me.' He'd told me the same thing when we were together, but I don't say that. 'He did take me on a trip to York once. Not for the rebellion, just for a day out. Not that there's much to do there now.'

I stiffen, remembering our own trip to York. He'd surprised me that day, knowing I'd wanted to visit all the dungeon attractions in the country, but I'd only ever been to the one in London. We had a really great day out. He'd picked us a hotel with a corner bathtub, too, which was amazing. I love baths. It was the first time we both said, 'I love you'. But I don't tell Celie this. Something inside me softens, knowing she's being just as fooled as I was when I started my relationship with James. I can't seem to hate her. And I have no reason to, not really. If she wants to be a bitch to me, that's her own issue. But I think she can come around.

165

'When did it all go wrong with you two?' she asks, bringing me out of my thoughts.

I frown. 'What do you mean?'

'Well, clearly he faked his death to get away from you. To not get you caught up in all this at the time. I know he cared about you. But you seem to hate him.'

I chew the inside of my cheek, thinking back to our whole relationship. It's hard to ascertain the tipping point. It seemed to happen all at once, out of the blue. I furrow my eyebrows, no, it didn't. There was one specific thing that changed it all.

'He missed my birthday,' I say, and Celie frowns. 'I know it sounds like a small thing, but that's when it started going downhill.'

'No, it's not that,' Celie says quietly. 'He missed mine, too. Didn't even wish me a happy birthday. I shrugged it off at the time. He's busy leading a rebellion after all.'

'Sure,' I say. 'And then after that, he'd never tell me where he was, or what he was doing and then tell me I was overreacting when I'd question him about it, and he'd get mad and give me the silent treatment.' Celie nods, giving me leeway to go on. 'And then he started getting texts in the middle of the night, wouldn't tell me who they were from. Something shifted in him, and he turned cold with me. It was like he hated me, and I couldn't figure out what I'd done to make that happen. And when I'd ask, he'd call me crazy and say I was overthinking again.' I take a deep breath. 'And then I went over to his one day, to confront him about it all. I'd had enough of him making me feel like that. And he was packing a bag, and then shoved me in the cupboard as the security officials came. As far as I knew after that, he was dead. I'd already had enough of it all, but it didn't stop me grieving. And that was it.'

Celie stares at me for a long time. I look away feeling slightly uncomfortable and she loses a breath.

'Thank you for telling me.'

I nod and she turns her back to me. I turn the light off above us. Talking for the night is over and we both need to sleep for whatever we're doing tomorrow.

'I think I've had enough too,' Celie says so quietly I almost miss it, like she doesn't even want to hear herself say it.

CHAPTER NINETEEN

The morning chill wakes us early. We eat a quick breakfast, then pack everything away.

'Grab a scarf to cover the bottom half of your face and put your gun under the back of your waistband,' Celie says coldly.

It doesn't look like last night changed anything. Her eyes are ringed with red, though I never heard her crying. I guess I slept properly for a change. With no light, I don't know how. I must have been exhausted. I don't mention her eyes.

'We're leaving the stuff here.'

I frown. 'Don't we need it?'

'Not where we're going. If we have time, we'll get it later.'

Still, she pulls on a small backpack that must have been stored in her bigger one.

'What's in that?' I ask, hoping she's prepared something for our lunch.

She shrugs it on without opening it. 'None of your business.'

I roll my eyes. Fine then.

We walk up the hill opposite the one we came down last night, then down and up, going on and on again.

'So many hills,' I say, out of breath. 'Can we stop for a second?'

Celie smirks at me. 'I thought after the trials you'd be able to handle a little hill.'

'First of all, this isn't a little hill. Second of all, that was about survival. Also, there were no hills.'

She shrugs. 'I didn't watch it.'

I throw my hands in the air. 'Then don't try to compare it.'

She stills. 'You're right, I'm sorry.'

I stand straight and put a hand on my chest in mock shock. 'What was that? I didn't think I'd ever hear you say sorry. For anything.'

She crosses her arms and looks at the ground where she kicks at a loose tuft of grass. 'Yeah, well, I realised last night you're not actually my enemy. James just wanted me to see you that way.'

'Then why are you still being a bitch to me?'

She raises an eyebrow. 'I'm a bitch to everyone, don't take it personally.'

I roll my eyes. 'Whatever. How far have we got left?'

'We've only been walking around forty-five minutes, so about three miles?'

All the walking I've done for this rebellion is making me wish I did have a step counter on my wrist. Trauma be damned.

I cringe.

It's not that easy.

'Let's get on with it then,' I say after catching my breath.

I can do another three miles. No problem. I almost stop. Three miles there. That means five miles back, plus that extra hill down to where the car is.

So, we walk.

We walk until we come to the top of yet another hill and we see a farmhouse below us on a stretch of fields. There are no sheep grazing, no chickens running around. No crops growing. Nothing that would suggest anyone lives here. And yet, there is movement in the house.

A man clad in the black uniform of a security official walks out of the front door.

'Shit, get down,' Celie says, and we both drop onto our fronts.

The security official doesn't even look our way as he walks to the side of the house, opening the wide brown door of the barn.

He isn't in there long before he exits, makes a call, then gets in a car and leaves.

There's no more movement in the house.

'We're going down there,' Celie says standing up and walking down the hill.

I scramble up behind her and grab her arm. 'Are you mad? What if there are more security officials down there?'

'There aren't,' she says, snatching her arm away and walking again. I follow this time. 'We've watched this place. There's only one man at a time who watches the place on the weekend. He just left; the next watch won't be here for an hour. You need to see what's inside that barn.'

'Fine,' I speak through breaths. 'But if they come early, I hope you have an escape plan.'

She pats the backpack and smiles. 'Of course I do.'

I roll my eyes but trust her. She wouldn't risk her own life.

We get down to the large barn. From inside, I can hear what sounds like machinery, which is odd. If they're not growing anything, what would they need it for?

We step inside. The machine I see has nothing to do with farming.

Before us is a long conveyor belt with four makeshift wooden coffins moving along. The lids of each coffin are nailed down. They all move towards what looks like an upgraded human body incinerator. Ashes spill from the other end into a large skip.

'What is this?' I ask, though I know. 'Why are they cremating bodies here.'

A thud comes from one of the coffins and I still. Someone is still alive.

'They're not bodies,' Celie says, confirming what I already know. 'They're all alive.'

My stomach drops. I try to process what she says. It doesn't make any sense. 'What? Why?' I ask.

I try to walk to the conveyor belt; I have to help these people. Nobody deserves to die like this. But Celie puts a hand on my shoulder, stopping me.

'You can't save them, Addy,' she says.

My mouth drops and I turn back to her. 'How can you say that? Is that not why we're here?'

She shakes her head. 'We don't have time. The next security official will be here soon. If we save them all, we won't get back to the car in time. We'll just die with them.' She pulls me back. 'Come on, you needed to see this, but I have to show you something else.'

I nod, leaving the barn with her. I knew the government were cruel, but I thought the trials and live executions were the furthest they were willing to go. This is inhumane. People need to know about this. Maybe then, we'd have a chance to change things.

Celie leads me outside where a massive rock towers over me, not unlike the ones at Stone Henge. On the rock is a metal board spanning the entire length with names etched into it.

Celie walks up to it, her finger trailing along the letter L. She gets to two names with the surname Liu and stops.

'My parents. My dad came here from China as a kid and married my mum in Sheffield. Weird that we're from the same place. Anyway, some of the security officials feel bad about what they're doing here and put their names on this board, so there's some memory of them.' She takes a deep breath.

'Why were they here?' I ask.

'People are brought here when they see something the government doesn't want us to know about,' she says through gritted teeth. 'I was there that day. We all saw what it was. What they wanted to keep hidden. They made me run when the security officials came, and I've been alone ever since.'

We're quiet for a moment as I let her breathe. It's always hard telling people what happened to your parents. I know all too well.

'I'm sorry,' I say eventually.

She raises a shoulder in a shrug and shakes her head. 'What's your last name?'

I frown. 'Taylor. Why?'

Her finger moves down to the Ts and stops on Elaine and Jack Taylor. My parents.

I suck in a breath. 'They were shot. There was a protest in town, and they were shot. Why would their names be here?'

'You were lied to, Addy. They were never shot. Did you ever hear about that protest on the news?'

My eyebrows furrow. 'No, but I was a zombie after they died. I didn't watch the news.'

'Well, it was never on the news. Because the person leading the protest was a lost member of the royal family. They still have supporters.'

I think back to my conversation with Lily and Gareth, about the secret royalists hiding in our faction.

I shake my head; it doesn't matter about the royalists. I don't care. I only care about my parents. 'No. No, you're wrong. They were shot. That's all. This can't have happened.'

'I'm sorry, Addy. I really am. I had the same reaction when I found out my parents were brought here. It's horrific.'

It's more than horrific. My mind fills with the sound of my parents helplessly banging on the lid of their coffins, begging to be saved. I had never thought much of the royal family, but I now hate whatever is left of them. I hope there are none left. My parents didn't deserve a death like that. Nobody does.

I nod, to myself more than anything, a decision being made. 'We can't let anyone else die like this.'

One side of her mouth lifts in a smile. 'Oh, we won't,' she says, but her smile falters. 'That's not all.'

My stomach drops. 'What else could there be?'

'Charmaine's parents are on the list.'

That stops me short.

'But they were escorted out of the county,' I say, frowning.

She shakes her head. 'Only people who could pay were allowed to leave. The rest were brought here.'

I sink to my knees, the thought of all our parents being brought here, locked inside a coffin, screaming as fire ripped into their bodies. I never knew where they'd been buried, was never given the option of a funeral. Now I know why.

'You know,' Celie says. 'They say the daughter of the royal guy who was leading the protest is still alive, somewhere out there. Building her own faction. Some say she's down south, in Dorset. But who knows if that's true.'

I barely hear her. I don't want to know about another royal. The pain of what happened to my parents is too loud for me to let anything else in. I put my fist in my mouth and scream against it, knowing I can't make a lot of sound in case the security official gets here early. The government have caused so much pain, so much death. They can't keep doing this. The pain radiating through my body stops and is replaced by the vibrations of anger.

This is exactly what James wants.

But right now, I don't care. They can't keep doing this, if I can be a small part of what will stop them, then I'll do anything. This week, I'll do what he asks, I'll find the trial centre.

I'll do anything.

I stand and stare into the horizon, across the hills with not a house in sight, and listen to the quiet. Not a single bird is in the air.

'My name is Adelaide Taylor,' I say. 'And I will not let them break me.'

I refuse. They've taken enough from me; they will not take anything else.

'That's right. Are you ready?' Celie asks.

I nod, knowing she's not asking if I'm ready to leave. But we start to, anyway. We walk back to the car, taking longer than two hours, going a different route, and not picking up our camping bits. I guess we don't need them.

Just as we get to the car, I notice something strange.

'Hey, where's your backpack?' I ask.

Celie smirks at me, takes her phone out of her pocket and presses a button on it. A loud bang followed by a crash, sounds from behind us somewhere in the distance. The shockwave from it reaches even us, knocking us to the ground and smashing the windows in our car. My hands graze and my ears ring as I turn over. A cloud of black smoke leaks into the sky.

I turn to see Celie shouting something to me and pointing at the car. I can't hear her over the ringing in my ears, but I grab the car door handle and pull myself up. There are pieces of glass on my seat, but I don't care, I just haul myself in. We speed away before anyone appears, and I'm sure they'll get there quickly.

The ringing subsides finally. My breathing slows, I didn't even realise it had sped up.

'What the fuck was that?' I ask.

'Well, Addy. It's what we like to call a bomb,' Celie says with a smirk.

'When did you even have time to plant it?'

She shrugs, her knuckles going white as she grips the steering wheel. Clearly, she's more afraid of us being caught than she's letting on. 'I just dropped the bag as we left the barn.'

I sigh. 'What do we do now?'

'Now? We lie low before going to London. You're allowed a sick day from uni, right?' I nod. 'Well, call in on Monday. We're staying in Sheffield until then. Home sweet home.'

I stiffen. I decided I would never step foot in my hometown ever again. The memories too painful. But it's the closest city to us, so it makes sense.

'Just as long as we stay away from Hillsborough.'

'Can do,' Celie says and looks at me. 'How do you feel after that?'

'Well, it was a huge risk, and I wish you'd told me.' I breathe out, my shoulders relaxing. 'But it was pretty amazing.'

She smiles at me, a wide toothy smile before she speaks. 'Welcome to the rebellion, Adelaide.'

CHAPTER TWENTY

We take a detour through Dronfield. We can't be sure if the security officials working last night saw our car or not, but we won't risk it. We get out of the car and walk thirty minutes until we find another sat outside a house that looks occupied. I stay outside as Celie sneaks in, coming out five minutes later with the keys.

'Were they not home?' I ask.

'They were, but they're an elderly couple and were having a nap on the sofa,' she says with a shrug. I grimace and she rolls her eyes. 'I left some money in the kitchen so they can buy another one, don't worry.'

That relieves me somewhat, but I still feel bad about stealing a car from vulnerable people.

'Why did you even have the money on you?'

'Emergencies, mostly. This felt like an emergency.'

I nod, accepting this as fact.

We drive the rest of the way to Sheffield.

The roads aren't as busy as they used to be on a Saturday afternoon.

I remember long car rides along the main road in Hillsborough when we'd catch the football match traffic. We'd lived here long enough to know when to avoid it, and how. But every now and then, after a long work week, too much exhaustion taking over, we'd forget to check online to see if one was on. It didn't help that I couldn't drive. I'd always chided myself for that. At least if it was just me driving home on a Saturday after work, I could blame myself. But my dad insisted he pick me up rather than me catching a tram and then a bus after being at work all day. And Saturdays at the vet clinic were always busier because that was the only day most people had off.

I miss that sometimes. The small moments with my dad in bad situations. At least it was time spent with him. I'd take that any day now.

We turn up the hill and drive through the woods of Grenoside until we come to a housing estate.

'We can stay at my house,' Celie says. 'I haven't been back for years, but as far as I know, nobody lives up here anymore.'

We drive onto her street.

Or what used to be her street.

She stops the car halfway up the road, and without turning the engine off she staggers out and through the gate to face the pile of rubble.

Heaps line both sides of the road. There are no signs left of what did this. Or why. A waste of resources when so many are homeless.

Another form of control.

Celie cries silently on the ground, tears staining her face.

I turn the car off and get out, wiping bits of glass off the back of my jeans. I feel a small sting as one of the pieces cuts me. But I don't care and just walk around to Celie.

I look around us, up and down the street, worried someone might come along and see us like this.

I put my hand on Celie's shoulder, gently. 'We need to go,' I say.

She looks up at me, trying to speak, but no words come out. She coughs, trying to find her voice.

'They took everything,' she whispers.

'That's what they do. You know that's what they do.' I crouch next to her. 'You just showed me how far they're willing to take things. This shouldn't be a surprise.'

She wipes her nose on the back of her sleeve and her face hardens. 'You're right. It's not. There was nothing worth coming back to in that house anyway. It was just a tomb for my memories.' She stands and walks back to the car but stops in front of it with a sigh. 'This will probably have been reported as stolen by now. We should change cars.'

'Alright. I used to live in Oughtibridge, we could walk down there for now. Find a car when we need to leave?'

She nods. 'Weird that we lived so close to each other. We could have known each other.'

'And yet, it was James who brought us together.'

'He knows something. I don't know what it is, but it has something to do with us. It's too big of a coincidence.'

I chew the inside of my cheek, thinking this over. She's right. What are the odds he'd find two people from the same city, let alone people who lived so close to each other? I don't know about Celie, but I know

I'm nobody special. There's nothing about me to know, to keep secret. I don't know what it could be.

We walk through the top of Grenoside woods. The trees give Celie some semblance of privacy and I move ahead of her while she pushes her emotions down. The crematorium still lies outside the woods, I notice. Funny that they didn't just use that to kill their victims. I turn my head away from it as we walk down the hill and I send a quick text to Isaac, telling him I'm fine but I won't be back until Monday. I tell him I'm back in Sheffield but not my exact location. The short amount of time I've turned my phone on will let whoever is monitoring it know we're here anyway. I just hope they can't pinpoint this exact location. He responds quickly with a *be careful*.

He doesn't tell me what he's learned this weekend, and that's fine, we need to keep communication short. I turn my phone off.

We get to the bottom of the huge hill leading out of Grenoside and into my village. I used to live just off the main road, so the rest of the walk is easy. Silent, but easy. I don't want to bother Celie with questions, not when she's just lost her final connection to her parents.

Instead, I try to come up with a plan for how to tell Charmaine. All she's had to hold onto is the hope that they would one day be reunited. What will this do to her? How far will it push her? I'm worried it'll force her to do something drastic, that James will use it to make her take a step she hasn't taken yet.

She hasn't killed anyone, that's what I do know. Not yet.

But this might be the thing that pushes her to do it, to take the life of someone in the government, to punish them for taking everything from her. From me. From all of us. So many of us are orphans, belonging to The Realm and no one else. *Children* of the Realm.

I finally understand why they call themselves that. Or rather, why *we* call ourselves that. I'm in deep with this now and I don't want to leave. Not until I have to.

'We're here,' I say finally as we stand in front of a dark brick terrace house. The noises of the neighbours echoing through my mind.

The street is silent, no cars littering it. Abandoned, but not yet destroyed.

We walk into the porch.

'Take your shoes off,' I say absentmindedly as I do the same.

Celie doesn't question me. The windows are covered in so much grime, I can't see out of them anymore. The kitchen is how I left it, tidy but with dust covering it. The cupboard doors stand open. People have been here. Raiding it for the food I left behind. I didn't see the point in taking it with me to the orphanage. But that's okay. There are shops close by. I know they're still open. Me and Charmaine would go into them whenever we failed to enter the psychiatric hospital up the road.

A shudder goes through me. I knew the orphanage was close to my old house, but I never really thought just *how* close. I tried to push it from my mind. It's all uphill, though. I don't need to go near it to get us food.

I lead Celie through the kitchen into the living room, with the old log fire. Both sofas are covered in sheets.

I close the blackout curtains and turn on the light, surprised to see that the electricity was never shut off. We both take the sheets off the sofas and sit down. It doesn't smell like home anymore. Damp has leaked in, and the air is musty.

I don't know where I belong.

'I'm going to turn the heating on,' I say. 'If it still works.'

The switch springs to life and allows me to turn it on. It takes a moment, but the pipes start to clang, signalling that heat will reach us. It'll take some time with how long it's been off, but we won't go cold tonight.

I light the fire in the living room for more heat.

'Do you want to go to the shop or should I?' I ask Celie.

She stands. 'I'll go. You...' She stops as she looks around. 'You should take a moment alone with all this. Where are the shops?'

I give her directions and she leaves.

My bedroom is in the attic so that's where I go first. Photos still hang on the wall, pinned up with fairy lights. Me and my uni friends captured in moments I'd forgotten about. Too much has happened to really care about it anymore. There's a photo of us dressed up like golfers during fresher's week, when we barely knew each other, but still went on a pub crawl together. We thought it was a friendship formed for life.

I don't know where they all are or what happened to them. I can only hope they survived when things turned bad. That they're doing more than just surviving now.

On the row of photos there's a small one of me and my cousin, Amy, when she came up from Poole to visit during first year. That was the last time I saw her. My mum, Amy's mum's sister, never heard from them either, as far as I know. They just disappeared. Maybe they're still living in the beach house in Poole. I'd like to think so anyway.

The door to my parents' room is still shut. I never opened it after they were taken from me, never took any of their belongings. It might as well be their mausoleum now, preserved perfectly in the way I wish they had been. If I keep the door closed then it's like they're in there, having an early night. I'll just tiptoe back down the hallway, down the stairs.

And I sit and wait in the empty living room. Empty of all life because I did take the photos in here with me to the orphanage. I kept a part of them with me. And they were taken from me all over again. The fire breathes on me, heating me from the outside in. Reminding me that I'm still alive, and, while I can never bring my parents back, I can do something about their deaths.

Celie returns with a variety of foods. The lock on the door is broken, so between us we move the fridge in front of it. We won't be here long enough to need it anyway. My stomach grumbles, reminding me that I haven't eaten for hours.

'What are we having then?' I ask, rummaging through the plastic bags.

'Scrambled eggs and beans on toast?'

I nod. 'Sounds good. Do you want me to make it?'

'It's fine, go sit down.' She searches the cupboards until she finds the pans and plates she needs. 'Does the TV still work?'

I go to check. I can't believe it's still here. I guess the people who raided the kitchen were just too desperate for food to steal anything else. It's outdated now anyway, I'm not sure anyone would buy it. The remote doesn't work, and when I check the batteries, they've rusted to it so that's no use. I find the "on" button on the bottom of the TV. All the old channels we used to watch disappeared when we stopped paying for them. All that's left are the big five. Well, that's all the aerial will pick up anyway.

I let the news play in the background, not bothering to pay attention.

Celie comes in with our food. We don't speak as we eat, swallowing each bite quicker than we probably should, but our pasts dictate our stomachs.

'That was good,' I say.

Celie just nods as she puts her plate on the floor then looks back up at the TV, her eyebrows furrowing. 'Can you turn this up?'

I do as she asks. On the TV we see the factory in Hope Valley, or what's left of it. The screen cuts to another bomb site in Wales. Then Scotland. More and more appear around the country. All at lunchtime today, almost at the exact time we blew up the factory. Finally, they show St Pancras train station. Blown from the tube tunnels beneath.

Celie's jaw drops, her eyes widen.

I frown. 'You didn't know this was happening?'

She scowls. 'Apparently there's a lot more that James isn't telling us.' Her voice falters. 'But I thought he'd at least tell me. I thought we were doing something huge, but we were just one out of a dozen. Nobody will even know what the factory was for now.'

'I'm sorry,' I say, if only to reply.

Her face turns to stone. She spins around to me. 'I do know something though, something he's been keeping from everyone. Especially you.'

'Why especially me?'

'I don't know. He just said you were important. Too important to lose—he'd always intended to find you again. There's something about you, about who you are that he needs on his side.'

I rub my face. 'I'm no one.'

She smirks. 'We both know that isn't true. You just need to figure out who you are. Anyway, that's not my point.'

'Then what is?'

'It's who James is that he's been trying to keep a secret.'

'And who is James?'

She pauses. For dramatic effect, or to decide whether she actually trusts me, I don't know.

She releases a breath I didn't realise she was holding. 'He's related to the Prime Minister.'

CHaPTer TwenTy-one

'You're not serious,' I say.

But my mind runs through our relationship again. How he never told me about his past. And I never did meet his dad. No wait, he said his dad was dead. And his mum seemed relatively normal. They were firmly middle class, and she'd remarried after his dad died. She seemed nice, but I don't recall her ever mentioning him. Was it even his real mum?

He didn't ever really talk about the past, what he did as a kid, where he went to school. And I only met his mum the one time. He'd change the conversation any time I'd ask about her again. His dad was completely off limits.

Celie's eyes sparkle in recognition as I realise all of this.

'So why is he doing all this?' I ask.

'Beats me,' she says with a shrug. 'Maybe his family didn't give him enough attention when he was younger. I don't know exactly how they're related, whether it's distant or what, but he thinks it'll help the rebellion in the long run. So, maybe he just has a giant chip on his shoulder. Have you ever noticed how he thinks the world owes him?'

I chuckle sourly. 'Absolutely, it's always been his way. If he doesn't get what he wants, he gets mad.'

I pick at a thread on the corner of the sofa, trying to think of what he's trying to accomplish. What his real parents could have done to him to make him want to rebel so much.

Celie's voice brings me out of my thoughts. 'Let's just be glad he's not the Prime Minister's son. He can never control the country.'

I shoot a look at her. 'What?'

'That was the law they made; the title is passed down like royalty unless the heir is unfit to take charge. They just can't rule alone like a royal can. They have their cabinet.'

I chew my lip, thinking. It doesn't really matter anyway. 'James wouldn't want to be Prime Minister anyway, right?'

She's silent for a moment, while she contemplates the question. I wonder how much he's actually talked about it to her, whether he's told her his real ambitions. She shakes her head and says, 'I don't think so. But I don't know if he wants change the same way we do.'

I sigh, I don't really know what to think. At least he's fighting for something, against what the government wants to do to us. 'Surely having him on our side is a good thing then?' I ask.

Her face turns contemplative. 'I guess we'll have to find out.'

We don't talk about James for the rest of the night, or the next day. And by Monday, the conversation is almost forgotten. Almost.

Before we leave, I gather all the photos from my old bedroom. Maybe I'll find Amy again one day. But until then, it'll be nice to have something from home. Some memories I can hold on to.

We steal another car and make the drive back to London. There are cars on the road this morning, all making a commute. But again, not as many as there used to be.

Celie drops me off at my flat and tells me to meet them at Covent Garden that evening. I walk in, fully intending to take an exceedingly hot shower, but before I can make it to my bedroom, Charmaine attacks me with a hug.

'I was so worried,' she says. 'I knew where you were going, and when I saw the news. I just—please don't do that to me again.'

'I won't,' I say, trying to escape her arms.

She pulls back and holds out her pinkie finger. 'Pinkie promise me. You can't break that.'

I roll my eyes, but link fingers with her. 'This is lame, but I pinkie promise I won't do it again.'

Her shoulders sag in relief.

'So, tell me everything,' she says.

I cringe and look up at all the cameras. With a sigh, I say, 'Fancy a walk?'

She frowns but nods and we both leave our phones behind.

We find our bench, where all these hard conversations seem to happen.

I chew the inside of my cheek so hard the metallic taste of blood explodes on my tongue. I listen to the wind whistle through the branches above us. Time has taken the leaves away from us quicker than I'd noticed. I try to find some calm in the noise, I'm finding it hard to say the words I have to.

Charmaine's face drops. 'What did you see there?'

I take a deep breath and tell her everything, about the factory, my parents and Celie's, what we did.

I pause for a moment, readying myself for what I'm about to say. 'But Charmaine, I need you to realise they're monsters. And you are not alone.'

She frowns. 'I know that.'

'But more than ever,' I say, holding onto her hand tightly. 'I love you and I won't ever leave you, okay?'

She rolls her eyes. 'Just tell me.'

'Your parents are dead.' There, I said it. I can never take it back.

She stills, her hand falling from mine. 'No, they're at home. In Barbados. I watched them go.'

I can't say it again, I can't take the one small sliver of hope she has left inside her. I choke on my words and tears begin falling.

'Their names were on the list.'

'Maybe there were other people with the same names.'

I look away from her, I need to be blunt, and I can't look at her. 'Charmaine, they're dead,' I say, my voice breaking.

'No. You're wrong,' she says, her voice coming out in barely a whisper.

My shoulders slump. She won't believe me. I can't even show her now, we destroyed the entire place.

My stomach tightens. James would know. Now I know who he is, it makes sense that he has all this insider knowledge. That he knows too much. He would know what happened to those supposedly sent back to their home countries. Whether they were made to leave or were killed.

'Come on,' I say, standing and dragging her along behind me.

'Where are we going?'

'To talk to James.'

She pulls her hand out of mine. 'Now I know you've lost your mind. James? *James?* What in the world would you need to talk to him about?'

I turn and run my hand through my hair. 'Look, I know how hard this is to accept. I didn't want to believe it about my parents either, but you have to believe me. Your parents are dead. I'm sorry.'

My voice comes out harsher than I intend, and something shifts in Charmaine's face.

'No,' she says. 'No, no, no, no, no.'

Her knees buckle, and I move to catch her before she slams to the floor. We both kneel there, alone except for the wind and the trees. A drop of water lands on my arm. Rain begins slowly, but I don't care.

I draw her into my arms, and she fists the back of my shirt. She screams into my shoulder, tears falling and wetting my t-shirt. The rain gets heavier, louder, covering the sound of her agony. She gulps breaths between sobs, and I can't help but cry with her.

We sit there for what feels like hours, long enough for her eyes to dry and her sobs to stop. Her face hardens in a look I've never seen before, and we stand. Her hair is flattened, and I can feel mine sticking to my neck. We're both completely soaked. It's like the sky opened up and cried with us.

'I'll make them pay for this,' she says.

I nod. 'I know, we need a plan. Let's go to the meeting.'

She shakes her head and wipes her nose on the back of her wet sleeve. 'You go, I just need to be alone for a while.'

She walks away before I can answer. I watch her back as she disappears from the path, turning away from the flats and walking faster until she's gone completely.

Did I just lose her?

After a short nap, I meet up with Isaac at Covent Garden. He came here straight from uni with Janesh and Ivy.

'Did I miss much?' I ask, interlocking my fingers with his.

He leans his forehead against me. 'No, but I missed you.'

He draws me in for a long kiss. A tingle runs down my spine as I press my chest against his. His hands clutch my hips, my sides, all the places he can while we're in front of people.

I break from the kiss, suddenly breathless.

'Later,' I whisper with a smile.

He just nods. 'Tell me what you learned.'

We move towards one of the beanbags at the back of the room, sitting as close together as possible. The warmth of his body soothes me, chasing away some of the anguish from the last few days as I tell him everything.

'How are you handling it?' he asks, pushing a piece of my hair behind my ear.

I avoid his eye, finding a spot on the wall behind the beanbags. It's bare except for one poster of a band that's still stuck to it. The corners have all started to curl in, and damp has made the information blend into each other. I don't know who the band were. I stare at it anyway. 'I'm fine.'

He raises an eyebrow. 'Don't lie to me.'

I look down at my hands, wringing my fingers together. I don't know why I tried to lie. 'Alright, I'm not fine. But I will be. Right now, that needs to be good enough. What did you learn?'

He sighs. 'April was part of James's faction.' My face falls. God, not his sister. 'She sacrificed herself, let herself be caught. She wanted to show the public just how awful the government were when they arrested someone below the age of eighteen for something they couldn't even prove. And then they lowered the execution age to sixteen. It was only her birthday a few days earlier. And she was the first one of her age to be executed live on TV. She was used as an example, and her sacrifice meant nothing. The general public just accepted it. And now it's fourteen. It's only going to get worse.'

I lean my forehead against his. 'We'll make them pay,' I whisper.

He lifts his lips to my head and kisses me quickly. 'I want that, I do,' he says with a sigh. 'But I don't want us to lose ourselves in the process. We can still get out of this.'

I lean back in shock. 'I can't Isaac, not now.'

He gives me a weak smile, pain shining through his eyes. 'Can you blame me for trying?'

Something tugs in my chest, and I wish so much that we could just leave. Leave all this, hell, even leave the country. But we can't. Not until this is over.

James claps from the table in the middle of the room, drawing us all in as the meeting begins.

'Where's Charmaine?' he asks of me.

'She's taking some personal time.'

He scowls but doesn't respond. Looking up at the rest of the group, he begins the meeting. 'This weekend was a success. We sent a message to the government; we could take them out at any time if we wanted to. But we won't, we didn't kill anyone with these bombings.'

'Why not?' Brendan says with a sneer. 'It's the least they deserve.'

James gives him a tight smile. 'Relax. We didn't kill anyone because we're not *them*. If, and when, we decide to do that, it'll be for the right reasons and motivations. Understood?'

Brendan nods.

The lift dings and Yu-Jun rolls out.

James raises an eyebrow at her. 'You're late.'

Yu-Jun is out of breath as she brings her chair closer. 'I know, I've been waiting. Hoping they'd check in, but they haven't.'

'Who?'

'Lily and Gareth. They checked in after they put the bombs below St Pancras. But I haven't heard from them since.'

James looks around the room, like he's just noticing part of his team is missing.

His face drops. 'They've been caught.'

CHAPTER TWENTY-TWO

J ames takes his phone out and starts calling people, asking if they've heard anything, where the two were last seen, if there's any chance they're still alive.

Celie puts a hand on his shoulder. 'We don't know they've been caught; they could just be hiding.'

James whirls on her, pushing her away from him. He uses too much force, and she falls to the floor. The room falls silent as we all gape at him. Isaac starts to move forward but I pull him back and shake my head at him, knowing Celie needs to take care of this herself.

James's mouth falls open, shocked at himself and he scrambles over to Celie.

'Celie—' he starts, an apology forming on his lips. Probably the first one he's ever thought to mutter.

She puts a hand out, stopping him. 'Don't! Don't come near me you fucking prick.' She stands, and nods at me before looking back at James. 'I'm done. With you, with this fucking rebellion. I'm out.'

Anger clouds James's face. 'You're not out until I say you're out.'

Celie laughs a humourless laugh. 'Whatever. But we're done. You can stop using me as your Addy replacement now. *Fuck you.*'

I frown at her words. We don't look anything alike; how would she be my replacement? But my face softens as I smile at her, encouraging her to leave.

James rolls his eyes. 'Fine. You were only good for a fuck anyway. Get out of my sight.'

Celie's eyes glimmer in anger as she turns to me. 'Remember what I told you,' she whispers. 'Don't trust him.'

She leaves the building. James doesn't even watch her go as he begins shouting demands at everyone to start searching for Lily and Gareth.

I step forward. 'What about us?'

He rolls his eyes. 'You're no use to me right now. You need to lay low until you can figure out where the boarding school is.'

Isaac steps in front of me. 'You ever touch a woman like that again and you're done.'

Sorrow fills James's eyes for a moment, like he actually regrets what just happened. But it's quickly replaced with something else that I can't quite place, but it fills me with fear as he laughs, gripping his stomach. 'Good one, Isaac.' His eyes flick to me. 'Threaten me again and you'll see who has the real power here.'

They glower at each other. Isaac is right, but this isn't our battle. Not right now, anyway. I tug on his arm.

'Come on, let's go home,' I say.

He slowly turns toward me, his face full of fury. I raise my eyebrows at him, challenging him, bringing him back to me, and his face softens. He links hands with me with a small smile.

'Sounds perfect,' he says, and we leave.

Janesh and Ivy follow us outside.

'I don't want to be part of that,' Janesh says. 'Lily and Gareth, James. Fucking James. It's too close. Why can't our lives just be normal?'

I can't believe he'd throw Lily and Gareth into a situation like that. Lily is so young. She's barely even started her life. I know we're all putting ourselves at risk, but wasn't there someone else who could do it instead? St. Pancras is too central. It didn't even need to be hit.

Janesh sinks to the pavement, his head in his hands, while I'm running through it all in my mind.

Ivy crosses her arms. 'Yeah, that was fucked up.' She shivers and looks up and down the street. Nobody is around. Nobody ever is in this part of the city. And nobody has followed us out. 'Any idea where Celie would go? We should check on her.'

I shake my head. 'Charmaine should have her phone number. You should come back with us?'

Her face falls. 'Why, what's wrong? I haven't seen her all weekend.'

I shake my head. 'She should be the one to tell you.' I glance down at Janesh. 'You two go ahead,' I say. Isaac gives me a quick kiss and they leave. I sit next to Janesh and bring my knees up to my chest, wrapping my arms around them. The ground is still wet, and I can feel it seeping through my jeans. 'You don't have to do this, you know.'

He looks up at me. 'I don't really have a choice.'

I frown. 'What do you mean?'

'James says he can get my dad out of jail and help us get out of the country. I think that's the only option for us now. I need to protect my family.'

I chew on my lip, contemplating the past few days. 'Janesh... do you know who James really is?'

His eyes darken. 'Do you?'

'I know who he's related to.'

The world around us is silent. We might be in the busiest city in The Realm, but everyone clusters in certain areas. Ruins of old shopping markets aren't exactly local attractions. We sit for a moment, listening to the quiet, watching the sky darken.

I miss seeing planes flying overhead, taking people abroad. I wonder what the world is like out there. I can only hope other countries have it better. Maybe Janesh will be better once he escapes.

'So, you see, he's my only hope,' Janesh says, finally.

My shoulders slump. 'I hope it's all over soon.'

Janesh looks at the sky, at the one star breaking through. 'Sometimes it feels like it'll never be over.'

I know what he means. This tyranny has been nearly six years of our lives. There's no end in sight. We don't even know what the rebellion would do if we managed to overturn the government. But anything is better than this.

'You've got something a lot of people in this country don't have,' I say, reaching over and gripping his hand.

'What's that?'

'Hope. Hold on to that.'

'It's not enough.' His eyes have gone distant, like he's planning something.

I give his hand a squeeze, bringing him back to the present. 'It has to be. Don't let them take that away from you.'

He nods and stands.

'Thanks, Addy. I don't deserve your kindness after everything I did in the trials. So, thank you.'

I stand and shrug. 'Winning the trials was all about getting a second chance, right? You deserve that as much as the rest of us.'

We hug and part ways.

I jog to catch up with Isaac and Ivy, linking my hand with Isaac's.

On the walk back to the flat, I tell them about James, who he really is and that we have to be careful. More than we have been. We don't know what his real motives are, but I can bet he'll be happy enough to throw us at the feet of the government if it served a purpose for him. I won't let that happen.

'You don't know how much I missed you this weekend,' Isaac says, between kisses.

He pulls my t-shirt over my head, and I kick my shoes off, finding his lips again quickly.

I unbuckle his belt, pushing his jeans down. He steps out of them. I run my hand along his thick, hard length and smile against his mouth.

'I think I can tell,' I say. He growls against my mouth and pushes me onto the bed. He takes my jeans and knickers off in one quick motion as I whip my bra off. His boxers follow and he hovers over me.

'Never again,' he says, pushing into me. 'We don't split up for something that dangerous ever again.'

He stills inside me. I touch his face, stroking along the stubble of his jaw and draw him in for a kiss as he pulls out, pushing back in with more force.

'Say it,' he says against my mouth.

'Together,' I say through a moan as he pushes into me again.

'That's right.'

He pulls my leg up to his hip, wrapping it around him. Locking him in place. As we move together as one, I know I don't want to be apart from him. This is forever.

I collapse against Isaac's chest, both of us done to completion—many times—and our skin glistens with sweat. His chest hair tickles against my face, and I rest my chin on it as I look up at him.

'I really love you,' I say.

His cock twitches inside me, hardening again.

He leans down for a kiss. 'And I really love you, Adelaide.'

I sit up, getting ready to move on him again when a knock sounds at my door, stopping us.

'Can you two stop fucking and put the TV on?' Charmaine shouts through the door.

I breathe out a sigh, not ready to let this go. Neither of us answer as we just stare at each other, his look flooding me with heat.

Charmaine groans through the door. 'I mean it, this is important. Addy, get off his dick and put BBC One on. Lily and Gareth have been found.'

I go cold. *Found*. If they're on TV, they weren't found by one of us.

'Okay,' I shout, climbing off Isaac and pulling his t-shirt over my head. I get under the covers, crossing my legs beneath me. Isaac sits up next to me and turns it on. 'The TV is on.'

'I'm coming in,' she says, barely giving Isaac enough warning to pull the covers up to his waist.

'Woah, that was not cool.'

'I don't care,' she says, Ivy following her. They sit on the end of the bed.

Ivy sniffs at the air. 'It stinks in here.'

I roll my eyes. 'Shut up and watch the TV.'

Prime Minister John Anderson stands behind his podium. The only resemblance he has to James is his dark hair and eyes. There's nothing in his face. I don't see how they could be related. But that doesn't matter right now.

Lily and Gareth are stood further back behind the Prime Minister on a raised stage, ropes loose around their necks. Their faces are covered with bruises. Gareth's right eye is swollen shut. Their hands are joined. They're the only people left of their family. It's bittersweet that they would be taken from the world together.

The Prime Minister begins, '*These terrorist attacks all over the country have been devastating. They have not only impacted the government, but public workers like you. We will not tolerate terrorism. And make no mistake, that is exactly what it is. An attack on the government and the country. The two terrorists behind me, after investigation, informed me of the name of their faction. They call themselves,* Children of the Realm.' A gasp escapes from me. I would expect them to talk after so much torture, but it's still a shock to hear the name spoken on live TV. '*As you can see, they are not children, nor are they representing The Realm. If you are part of this faction, please come forward. Those between eighteen and twenty-five will be given the option to compete in the trials. The rest will have a long life in prison, but you will not face execution. Lily and Gareth Grey will not be given that second chance. Terrorists do not deserve a second chance. They will be executed now.'*

He steps away from the podium and nods at the two. *'Any last words?'* he asks, conceding one small act of kindness.

Gareth says nothing, but Lily clenches her jaw. '*Your time is over, we will succeed.* Children of the Realm *are coming, and you cannot stop us, you cann—'*

The Prime Minister stops her speaking, nodding at the executioner. He pulls the lever and the floor below Lily and Gareth drops.

They let go of each other as they claw at their necks, the drop not strong enough to break them. Their faces turn red, then purple as they suffocate. Gareth gives in first. Lily looks over at him between chokes, tears streaming from her eyes, and a look of anger crosses her face. In this moment, she reminds me so much of the girl who was executed when the trials were announced. This is almost exactly the same situation. The Prime Minister asking for volunteers of a different kind to compete to their deaths.

Lily closes her eyes and stops struggling, succumbing to the darkness. Their bodies sway in the wind as a heavy rain starts, battering them, washing their souls away.

Nobody will come forward after that.

CHapter Twenty-THree

The next day, I go back to uni. Everything feels normal, but it isn't. Helen notes my absence from the day before and says she hopes it won't happen again. I tell her it won't as long as I keep up with my counselling. She gives me a tight smile, clearly not happy that I'm using my mental health as an excuse. It might not be only her fault, but she's partly to blame for the trauma I've faced.

With Christmas just over a week away, and the trials for the next month chosen, we're free to go wherever we want in the uni to study for exams and to complete our final assignments of the semester. I still don't understand any of the subject. I want to study something else, to become a vet like I had wanted to all those years ago. Hell, I'd even take English Literature over this.

At lunch, we sit with Ivy and Janesh.

'How are you doing today, Janesh?' I ask quietly.

'Better. Thank you for talking to me.'

Ivy speaks up. 'I spoke to Charmaine last night. She told me about her parents. I'm so angry for her. They just take and take, and nobody ever does anything about it.'

I look around us, trying to see if anyone heard what she said. 'Keep your voice down. This isn't the place to discuss this, and you know it.'

She breathes out. 'I know, I just feel angry all the time now. Don't you?'

I glance at Isaac, a spark of happiness lighting up his eyes and my cheeks flush. 'Sometimes, yeah,' I say. 'But I'm trying to focus on the good things.'

'I get that, but you can't be so ignorant to believe you can escape it.'

I clench my jaw, irritated. 'That's not what I said.'

She shakes her head. 'I want to *do* something. Be part of something. Instead of just learning to fight. What good is that right now? At least you got to do something at the weekend. Was it just amazing?'

I can't help but grin. 'Yeah, okay, it was pretty amazing. But just wait. I can feel something coming.'

And I can. James won't have taken the news last night lightly, he'll be plotting something big now. I just hope we survive it. I just hope we survive him.

'Are you still having the nightmares, Adelaide?' Caroline asks me. It's Thursday and our fourth counselling session so far.

I'm sat in the leather-bound chair, facing her at her desk as she types in notes whenever I speak. I don't know what she does with them. All I can do is hope she isn't sharing them with Helen.

'Sometimes, yeah,' I respond. 'Less so when I have company.'

'Isaac, yes? You met him during your trials?' I nod. 'And there's no trauma there? I'd have thought he would be a reminder of it all.'

I can't help picking at my nails. I really don't want to be here. 'No, he was the only light I had through the entire thing. Sometimes he still is.'

'I see. And you sleep with the light on, even with him there?'

'The bathroom light yes, with the door partially open.'

'You're a little old to be scared of the dark.'

I shrug. 'There are monsters out there in the dark. Just ask Brett.'

'Yes, I remember that well. You must know that was manufactured though?'

'It doesn't stop the nightmares.'

She takes her glasses off, clasping her hands in front of her.

'I'm not here to judge, I hope you know that.'

'I know.'

She raises an eyebrow at me like she doesn't believe a word I say. 'With the Christmas break coming next week, we won't see each other again for a while.' She makes a few notes on the computer and the printer behind her springs to life, spitting out a green sheet of paper. 'I'm prescribing you an antidepressant that will help you sleep in the meantime. It won't completely stop the nightmares, but it'll get you to sleep when you feel like you can't.'

I take the prescription from her. 'Will you be telling Helen about this?'

She gives me a soft smile. 'I shouldn't think it's any of her business, do you?'

I smile back. 'Not at all. Thank you.'

I leave the office, meeting Isaac outside. We direct our car to the pharmacy close to home, that just so happens to be a few streets away from the library we want to go to.

'Are you really going to take them?' he asks as we leave the pharmacy.

I shrug. 'What harm could it do?'

'None, I guess. It's just that nobody really gets given antidepressants anymore.'

'That's less to do with the drug being bad and more to do with people being unable to afford them. We're lucky we can now. Otherwise, we'd be fucked for birth control.'

He chuckles. 'Yeah, I don't think we could cope with an accident like that right now.'

'Oh?' I look up at him with a smirk. 'You don't think we could juggle uni, the rebellion, *and* a baby? I think we're equipped for anything.'

He wraps his arms around my waist kissing my forehead. 'I would love to have kids with you.'

I smile up at him, kissing him quickly. 'Me too. Let's just get through the little life we have right now first.'

'Agreed.'

We walk hand in hand to the library. We have about half an hour before it closes. It reminds me of the one in the boarding school, with the directory at the front and the shelves lining so far back I can't see them all. Ironic considering the boarding school is exactly what we're looking for.

We go to the section with the books on schools in the area, but none of them are boarding schools.

'Well, we tried at least,' I say.

Isaac's face hardens. 'We can't give up, this is our final test, right? So, James clearly knows it's possible.'

'Yeah, but how?'

We leave the library, the librarian closing up behind us. We walk along the empty streets for a while before continuing our conversation.

'I think they're already setting it up. They must be with all the trials getting ready. What if we borrow a car from James tonight, drive ourselves to uni in the morning and follow Helen after?'

I stop, tugging Isaac back. 'That's an insane plan.'

He shrugs. 'We could do it though.'

I roll my eyes. 'And if we get caught?'

'We won't.'

'But if we do?'

'Then we're doing it as part of your healing. *Our* healing. We just want to see where it all started. To normalise it.'

I think it over, the plan is completely insane. But our reasoning if we get caught could be explained away as two people with trauma.

'Alright then,' I say, leaning up to kiss him. 'But if we get caught then that's it, okay? We're out. We have to be.'

He nods. 'Absolutely, we don't risk anything more.'

We change directions to Covent Garden, to pick up the car we'll need for tomorrow. I feel sick, and I can't decide what the feeling is about. But as my stomach begins to fill with dread, I can't help but think we might lose each other in this rebellion.

But I won't let that happen tomorrow.

CHAPTER TWENTY-FOUR

J ames lets us borrow a car that evening, but not without a lecture about staying hidden and being careful.

'If you get caught, you're on your own,' he says, his face bored like he doesn't really care whether we survive this or not. 'Report back as soon as possible. I'm sure I don't need to tell you to turn your phones off.'

I roll my eyes. 'Of course not. I don't even know why we have them at this point.'

James gives me a smug look. 'Well, Addy, wouldn't it look strange if the winners of the trials were suddenly unavailable to the government? You need to be accessible for them to use you at any given moment.'

My shoulders slump. He's right, of course. But they must know we don't have them when we leave the flat, considering the cameras they installed. Maybe they just want to give us a little bit of privacy. I laugh inwardly. When have they ever cared about that?

We go through the next day at uni, the last day of the semester, hardly listening to either of our friends. Barely even talking to each other as we sit and think over the plan for this evening.

Once uni lets out, we sit in the car park, watching the doors, waiting for Helen to leave. Darkness creeps in around us. Cars leave, but still, she stays. Lights won't be turned off. No, the students living here can come and go from the classrooms, libraries, and canteen all night. It's only the offices that will be locked.

Finally, she exits the building, her phone between her shoulder and ear. We can't hear what she says, but a flash of anger crosses her face. A car pulls up in front of her, the driver gets out and opens the back door. We wait thirty seconds after they've left to follow them. There's only one road out of this place anyway.

James told us to always stay the length of a few cars behind them, so that's what we do. We exit onto a busier street, but always have our eyes locked on them.

'How far away do you think the school is?' I ask.

Isaac grips the wheel a bit tighter. 'I don't know, but it can't be that far, right? It didn't take hours to get there from the train station when we started our trials.'

I nod absentmindedly. I can't remember much of that journey. Just the excitement between me and Celeste. When we both thought we had a flashy new life ahead of us. Before we knew all too well what the consequences of failure would be.

'It feels like a lifetime ago sometimes,' I say, wishing Celeste was here with us.

I don't know if she'd have been part of the rebellion. She was kind, too kind to be taken like she was. My throat tightens, the memory of her alive in my mind forever.

'I know what you mean,' Isaac says after a few moments. 'It was less than a year ago, but so much changed during them. So much has changed since them.'

He rests a hand on my thigh, and I smile slightly.

'Do you ever wonder where we'd be now if we didn't volunteer for them?'

He frowns, his hand tightening on my thigh slightly. 'We'd have been miserable, even more so than we are now, I think.'

I nod. 'So much loss and death to get us here.'

'So much more to come.'

I stiffen, but he's right. There's no end to everything, to The Realm, without it. I just never thought I'd be playing such a big part in it.

We spend the next forty minutes in silence. A sheet of dread settles over me, attaching itself deeply into my skin, making sure I won't escape it any time soon. The six months between the end of the trials and uni starting were so hard, but sometimes, I wish I could go back to it. To being ignorant of everything around me. To having no responsibilities.

But that would be selfish. I'm here now and I want to make a difference.

'There,' Isaac says, bringing me out of my thoughts.

I look up and watch the car turn down a long, secluded road, surrounded by woods. The sign for Edgewood Boarding School at the end of the road. We don't follow though, driving past.

'What are you doing?' I ask.

'We can't follow them this way. They'd know they were being fol-lowed.' He pulls off at the side of the road and gets out of the car, grabbing a backpack out of the back. 'We need to go through the woods, on foot.'

'In the dark.'

He smiles slightly. 'I know, not ideal, but it's our only way now.'

I sigh and get out of the car. 'At least tell me you brought torches.'

He pulls two out of his bag. 'What do you take me for?'

'Alright, but do not let go of my hand.'

'Wouldn't dream of it,' he says, locking his fingers with my own.

I grip him tightly as we enter the woods. Darkness envelops us and my breathing quickens. It feels so much like those nights in the first trial that I almost stop Isaac. I almost ask him if we can just leave. If we really need to do this at night, now we know where we're going. But I won't. We've come this far now that I can't give up. Otherwise, what were the last few weeks about?

I push my fear down completely, but I'm sure it'll come back when I go to sleep. Brett's death lingers through my mind as we delve deeper through the woods. I can't stop imagining what could be hiding, waiting for us to step in front of them so it can take us down.

The trees seem to grow above us, blending so far into the sky I don't know where they stop. Our feet crunch the leaves covering the ground. Frost is starting to set in with the cold and I wish I'd worn more layers. The black winter coat I wore is great for stealth but isn't the best for the ice.

We don't speak, the only sounds we make are our quick breaths. A cold wind screams through the trees, pushing us along the path as an owl follows us. The crickets sing their nightly song, letting us know we're not alone. That we're trespassing on something else's territory. It's never-ending. The torches light the path in front of us, but I can't see for the miles around us. I feel sick, my mouth tastes like blood, and I just want to leave. A buzzing sounds in my head, letting me know my anxiety has arrived and I grip Isaac's hand tighter.

'I'm here,' he says.

I don't reply but something eases in my chest slightly. We walk on, for twenty, thirty minutes. I'm almost certain we're lost when I see the faint flickering of a light between a gap in the trees before us.

I breathe a sigh of relief and we both quicken our pace. Stealth the last thought on our minds as we see more and more lights, the windows in each of the buildings showing life inside.

The buildings themselves appear and my breath is taken from me like I've been punched in the gut.

'We shouldn't be here,' I say.

Isaac looks back at me, worry clouding his face. 'You're right, but we need to see it now.'

I nod and let him guide me to the treeline. On the footpaths we once walked are people around our age going from the hall to the dorms. But they're not alone. Behind each group walk three security officials, their guns ready for who knows what. I shrink back into the trees.

'I didn't realise they'd already started bringing their criminals here,' I whisper.

Isaac shakes his head. 'We should find out how long they've been here, James would want to know.'

He starts to walk forward but I grip his hand, pulling him back as a memory flashes before my eyes.

To the right of the path is a forest, and I can't help but look into it. I meant what I said about feeling connected to it. It always calms me. Out of the corner of my eye I see something, or someone, move in the trees, but when I turn to look properly, nothing is there.

During our first trials here, one of James's underlings was watching us. Charmaine all but confirmed it when she first tried to recruit me.

'James knew,' I whisper harshly.

Isaac's eyebrows furrow. 'Knew what?'

'Knew where this was. He already knows.'

Realisation crosses Isaac's face. 'Then why are we here?'

'To test our loyalty? To get us caught and out of the way? I don't know.'

'He could have just turned us in himself.'

'And face questions about how he knew what we were doing?' I shake my head. 'He wouldn't risk it, wouldn't risk his own safety. Only everyone else's.'

Isaac's face hardens. 'We need to leave then.'

My stomach clenches. 'Back through the woods?'

'It's the only way.'

I nod, resolve running through me as we turn back to the darkness.

'Hey!' A voice sounds from behind us, and we freeze. 'Turn around. Now.'

We turn slowly. A security official stands on the grass before us, his gun raised. We both drop our torches and raise our hands in surrender.

'We don't mean any trouble,' Isaac says.

'Who are you and what are you doing here?'

I step forward. The security official tightens his hands on the gun, and I stop. 'I'm Adelaide Taylor and this is Isaac Webb.' Recognition crosses the security official's face. 'We were in the first set of the trials, we won them.'

'That doesn't explain why you're here.'

I freeze. It doesn't, but I don't want to explain myself to him. I want to run. But that's a one-way ticket to a bullet in the back of my head.

I gulp, my throat tightening. 'I just needed to see the place.'

Is that sympathy that crosses his face? I don't know, it's gone too quickly.

He lowers his gun and speaks into the walkie-talkie attached to his shoulder.

He straightens. 'You can lower your hands. Follow me.'

We do as he says, and he leads us to an all too familiar building. Helen told me I'd passed my exams here and I was moving onto the two weeks of training. Nothing has changed in the hall. The security official knocks on the door and Helen's voice sounds from within.

'Come in,' she says, and we enter. She looks up at the security official from her seat behind the desk. 'You can leave us.'

He bows his head slightly—*bows?* —and leaves, shutting the door behind us.

Helen sighs and gestures to the two chairs in front of her. 'Sit please.'

We do as she says. I try to speak. 'Miss Hale—'

She holds her hand up, stopping me. Anger clouds her face. 'I can't say I'm not disappointed in both of you. What exactly do you think you're doing here?'

I pick at the ends of my nails and look down at my hands. 'Just with everything going on right now, my trauma from the trials, the nightmares, I just needed to see the place again. I needed to know it was real. Isaac came with me, but this is all on me.'

She sighs. 'Be that as it may, you had no right. The stupidity of you both coming here. Risking the integrity of the trials. I should report you to the Prime Minister.'

I stiffen. If she does that, it's all over for us.

She leans back in her chair and crosses her arms, tapping her nails on one arm, thinking. She breathes out. 'I'm not going to do that, so wipe those miserable looks off your faces.'

I didn't realise I looked so worried. I harden my face, trying to look less like the emotional wreck I can feel myself becoming.

She smirks, knowing she has so much power over us. 'You will both be on academic probation, and this will be added to your record. Step one toe out of line and I will change my mind. And then your fates will be out of my hands. Count yourselves lucky that today wasn't a planned visit for the Prime Minister.' She takes out her phone, typing a quick text. 'You can go. A car is waiting at the gates for you.'

We stand and leave.

'Thank you, Miss Hale,' I say.

Her face tightens. 'Don't thank me. Just don't be so stupid again.'

I nod and we leave. Our shoulders relaxing.

That was far too close. We let the driver take us home, he doesn't say anything to us, and we don't talk to each other. The stupidity of letting James tell us what to do really sinking in now.

When the car drops us outside our building, we stop for a moment before entering.

'I think we need to be done,' Isaac says. 'This was too much, too close.'

I nod. 'You're right. Tomorrow, we'll tell James we're out.'

'If he lets us leave that is.'

I grimace. 'He has to, I can't do any more of this. Ivy was right the other day. All I feel right now is anger. If I keep doing what James tells us, I'll let the anger win and I don't know what will happen if I do that.'

He pushes my hair behind my ears. 'I won't let that happen. If he doesn't let us leave, then we run. Leave all of this.'

I smile. 'You'd really leave everything behind?'

'For you? I'd do anything.'

I wince. 'Let's hope it doesn't come to that. Not with Helen watching us.'

CHapTer TwenTy-Five

The next day, we go to Covent Garden, ahead of our scheduled meeting. Isaac grips my hand tightly. I chose not to tell Charmaine about what happened last night, about our plans. I'll tell her after if I have to. She was snuggled on the sofa with Ivy asleep in her lap and I didn't want to ruin such a perfect picture of peace.

James is already there, speaking with Yu-Jun about the security of the next mission. I try not to listen but can't help but hear him mention how many people will be in place for it. At least one hundred. I didn't even know he had that many people following him.

I cough, interrupting his conversation.

'We'll continue this later,' he says.

Yu-Jun looks up at us and raises an eyebrow. She just shrugs. 'Fine, but we don't have a lot of time.'

James sighs. 'I know. Leave it with me.' She leaves and James turns to us. 'So, tell me. How did it go?'

I clench my jaw. 'Did you set us up?'

His eyes widen in surprise. 'What do you mean?'

'Helen caught us. And I know you already knew where the school was. You were having it watched during the first trials.'

He rolls his eyes. 'Yes, I already knew where it was. What would be the point in trusting the two of you to find out something so important just for the sake of a test?'

'We were caught, I assumed you had something do with that.'

Anger clouds his face. 'It's not my fault you're both idiots. Why are you here if you think I'd set you up?'

'We came to tell you we want out.'

He rolls his eyes. 'Not possible. You're too important to the cause now.'

'Why?'

'As winners of the last trials, your faces are invaluable. If you're leaving, it'll be in body bags. Your deaths will make you martyrs.'

The shock of what he says takes me back and I can't speak. It's almost like that's exactly what he wants to happen.

He smirks but Isaac steps forward. 'That's ridiculous, what's the point in us doing all this if you just plan on killing us?'

James feigns shock. '*I* wouldn't be the one killing you.' But his eyes flick between us, telling me something, but I don't know what. 'And I don't plan on you dying. I don't plan on any of us dying, but it's a risk we all take, isn't it?'

Isaac clenches his fists. 'A risk we don't want to take anymore.'

James rolls his eyes. 'You're both acting irrationally because you got caught once. And look at you, you got away, didn't you? Something big is happening next week, on Boxing Day. But if you're both going to be such wimps about it, you can sit this one out. I don't need anyone there who won't pull their weight.'

My shoulders relax. Isaac looks at me, a question in his eyes about whether we should accept this. I nod. I don't think we have much of a choice anyway.

'Fine,' Isaac says, turning and grabbing my hand.

'Oh, and Addy,' James says before we leave. I bite the inside of my cheek and look at him. 'Try not to let him get you caught again.'

'He didn't—'

'You already know I have eyes everywhere. I know it was all his idea.'

'You're a prick.'

He smirks. 'So I've been told.'

Isaac turns back. 'Leave her the fuck alone, or I'll make you.'

A cold smile takes over James's face. 'I warned you not to threaten me again. Now, leave.'

We leave and walk back to the flat.

Isaac is silent, his jaw clenched in deep thought, and I stop him.

'It wasn't your fault you know,' I say.

He runs a hand through his hair. 'If I didn't try to take us closer, if we had just left when you wanted to, the security official wouldn't have found us.'

'That's ridiculous. We barely moved from the tree line; he saw us as soon as we turned to leave.'

'We shouldn't have been there in the first place.'

'No, but we were, and it's done now.' He looks over my head, so I rest a hand against his cheek. 'Look at me.'

He does, but anger still clouds his eyes. 'Do you want to run?'

He shakes his head. 'Not yet. I want to know what they've got planned for Boxing Day.'

I sigh, admitting defeat. 'Yeah, but we can't get involved this time.'

'I just want to do something before we disappear, be a part of something.'

I nod. 'There's something wrong with James though. I don't think he's doing this for the right reasons. Not for the same ones we are.'

'I think he wants power.'

I still. 'How would he even get that?'

Isaac shrugs. 'We'll see next week.'

We continue walking, not speaking about disappearing again. On the way back, I take some more cash out of the ATM. I have thousands saved now, enough to get us away if—*when*—we need to run.

But I don't tell Isaac that, I won't tell anyone that. I don't want to risk anyone else, if it looks like I'm getting ready to run, I'm already in danger.

We spend the week holed up in my room, only leaving for food, our uni assignments forgotten. When we made the decision not to run, we decided to make the most of every moment. I know Charmaine and Ivy are doing that, too. There's something bad in the air. An impending doom floating around us. I've asked Charmaine what is happening, but she won't tell me. She says it's too dangerous for me to get involved and to just let it go.

But if it's too dangerous for me, then it's too dangerous for her.

On Christmas Eve, I take my antidepressants. It doesn't feel like Christmas Eve anymore. Not the way it used to, when I was excited to wake up the next day and watch my parents opening their presents, the look of thanks written across my mum's face before she even knew what she had. I'd do themed presents each year, whatever their interests were at that time. After the pandemic, I made my mum a huge self-care kit. She took some time off work to finally get the sleep she hadn't gotten for years. I'd give anything to go back to that day, the end of what we thought was the worst period of our lives. Little did we know what was to come.

The tablets knock me out and I have no dreams, no nightmares about the woods or Celeste.

I wake on Christmas Day to Charmaine jumping on my bed. I struggle to open my eyes, a groggy feeling taking over my body. But Charmaine has so much energy that I force myself awake. Force myself to sit up and rub the sleep from my eyes.

'Are you awake?' she asks.

'I'm sat up, aren't I?'

'That doesn't mean you're awake.'

'Is anyone without coffee?'

'Do you want one? I'll get you one.' She rushes out of the room before I can answer her. I raise my arms in a stretch, my knees clicking as I push my feet out. I can't tell if I had a good night's sleep because I still feel so shit.

Charmaine returns to my room, two mugs in her hands and gives me one.

I take a long sip, scolding my tongue, but it wakes me up more.

Charmaine is grinning at me. I don't think I've ever seen her this happy.

'Did you just have some great sex or something?'

'Don't be so bitchy,' she says, whacking my leg with a sigh. 'No, Ivy is with her family today. She said her siblings wanted her to wait up with them for Santa, so I'm all alone.'

I chuckle. 'You're so dramatic.'

'Says you.'

I roll my eyes. 'I haven't had a chance to get your present out yet.'

'Totally fine, open yours first please.'

She hands me a cube-shaped box and I put my coffee on the bedside table. She watches me unwrap the glittery paper, a sparkle in her eye.

Inside is a moon lamp. My jaw drops.

'How did you even find this?' I ask. They stopped selling them years ago.

She shrugs. 'I am a master of secrets; I can find anything.'

I stiffen at her words. 'A master of secrets indeed.'

She sighs. 'Don't start again. I told you, it's too dangerous.'

'If it's too dangerous for me, then it's too dangerous for you.'

She rolls her eyes. 'Don't worry about me,' she says, tapping me on the nose before jumping off my bed. 'Have a shower and dress in something pretty. I'm making us a breakfast buffet seeing as we're waiting for Isaac to have Christmas Dinner.'

I laugh. 'Oh my God. Do you realise we're accepting the southern use of the word dinner by having it in the evening?'

A look of shock crosses her face. 'How dare you say something so blasphemous. No. I will never accept it.'

I shrug. 'You were the one who said it.'

'I retract my statement. It's Christmas Tea. Forever and always. Now get ready.'

We spend the day together, eating so much breakfast food and watching DVDs I found in the back of charity shops. The ones they're not supposed to sell. They only take cash for things like that, so there's no trail if we ever get caught.

It's the most normal thing I've done in what feels like months. I didn't realise I could feel normal anymore.

Charmaine leaves the sofa at five to start making tea.

I stretch back, rubbing my belly. 'I don't know if I could eat another thing you know.'

She glares at me. 'You'd better. This is our new family so this is a family meal. Next year, we'll have Ivy too.'

I sigh, getting up to help her. 'What will next year even look like? I don't think about my future anymore, it's so unpredictable.'

Her shoulders slump as she peels the potatoes. She shakes her head. 'Hope, Addy. Hope that eventually every day will be like this. Boring and normal.'

I smack her arm. 'Are you saying my company is boring?'

She laughs. 'No, but don't you think it'll be boring to not be worrying about our deaths constantly?'

I chew the inside of my cheek. 'Yeah, I hadn't thought of it like that actually. But it'll be *nice*.'

'My English teacher hated that word. But I agree.'

Isaac chooses that moment to knock on the door and I open it, a smile on my face. He lifts his arms, showing the five bags he has in his hands. 'I brought gifts.'

'For how many people?' I ask with a laugh, giving him a quick kiss and dragging him into the flat.

'Who knows when we'll get to celebrate like this again, let's enjoy it,' he says, putting the bags on the table.

He draws me in for a longer kiss, the sound of Charmaine gagging making me smile against his lips.

But I can't smile for long. Something about what he said, about enjoying *this*, fills me with dread.

CHAPTER TWENTY-SIX

We all sit around the table to eat the Christmas tea. Isaac regales us of how it was at his parents' house. They made the best of what they could. It was easier than last Christmas, but the first one is always the worst. I don't think his home will ever be the same without April there. I wonder if his parents will decide to move.

'Shall we do a cracker then?' I ask Isaac and his face lights up.

'Definitely, we didn't have any at home. In fact, they barely even decorated.' His face falls. 'I think because it's just the two of them now, they didn't see much point. It felt empty without April.'

I run my thumb over the back of his hand. 'I'm sorry, Isaac,' I say. 'I hope our decorations make up for it somewhat.'

'They absolutely do,' he says, looking up at the tacky streamers reaching from each corner of the ceiling to the centre of the room. He gives me a kiss and holds up his cracker. 'Ready?'

I grab my end and we pull, a loud pop echoing through the room.

'That was loud,' Charmaine says. 'Please, no more.'

I stick my bottom lip out. 'But I want a paper crown.'

She rolls her eyes. 'Fine, but let's do ours together so we can get it over with.'

I laugh as I obey, a purple crown falling out of mine.

'For tonight, we are royalty. The new royal family of The Realm of Great Britain.'

Charmaine concentrates on her mash potatoes. 'Right. Exactly. That's us.'

I frown. She's acting weird again. But I'm not about to let that ruin my day.

We finish our food, stomachs full to the brim and sit down on the sofa. Isaac puts his arm around my shoulders, and I lean into him. Content for once.

I'm just dosing off when I hear the sound of vibrating and Isaac shifts under me. I sit up slightly blurry eyed.

He takes his phone out of his pocket and frowns at the unknown number. 'Who would be calling me on Christmas day?'

I shrug. 'Dunno. You'd better answer it though.'

He nods and presses the green phone button, lifting it to his ear. 'Hello? Yes. What?' He looks down at me. 'Yeah, one second.' He shifts himself off the sofa and puts the phone to his chest, muffling the microphone. 'I need to take this in the hall.'

'You can just use my bedroom,' I say.

'It's fine, I'll be two minutes.' He leaves the flat.

I sit watching the door.

Charmaine nudges me and I jump. She hasn't spoken for so long, I forgot she was even in the room.

'You okay?' she asks.

'Yeah,' I say. 'That was weird, wasn't it?'

She lifts one shoulder in a shrug. 'Maybe. I'm sure he'll tell you what it's about when he comes back in.'

The door opens again, and Isaac walks back in. His face is blank and he's walking a little stiffly.

'You okay?' I ask.

'Fine,' he says. 'Just full.'

'Who was on the phone?'

'What? Oh, my mum. She just wanted a private word with me.' I raise my eyebrows at him, and he gives me a tight smile. 'It's fine, don't worry.'

But I am worried.

I sit back against the sofa, my shoulders tense. Isaac doesn't move to draw me to him. He doesn't sit back. He starts tapping his foot. I look at Charmaine with a frown, but she just shrugs and looks at her phone. Isaac bites at his nails. It's like he's waiting for something. But what? Who was really on the other end of that phone call? He'd have his mum's number saved.

The door slams open, and my breath is pushed from me as we all stand up and back away. A group of security officials stride into the room.

'Isaac Webb,' the man at the front says. His helmet covers his face completely.

Isaac stands straight, facing him head on. 'That's me.'

'You have committed treason and must therefore suffer the greatest punishment.'

Death. Death is the greatest punishment.

Without thinking, I move in front of Isaac. I'm out of breath, the wind knocked from me so quickly I can't catch it.

But I manage to speak as the man walks forward. 'Wait.' I put my hand up and he stops. 'What treason? What has he done?'

'You risked the integrity of the trials. This is a warning for you and the other winners. If you do not move, you will be arrested.'

'Where are you taking him?'

Isaac puts his hand on my shoulder, turning me around. 'Addy, let them take me.' His eyes penetrate me, trying to communicate something, but I don't know what. He lets out a sigh. 'Just trust me, okay? I love you.'

He kisses me quickly then pushes me behind him.

'I'm ready to go,' Isaac says and steps forward, his hands together in front of him, awaiting handcuffs.

'Isaac, no!' I say through a sob. I can't let him go. He hasn't done anything wrong. Nothing more than what I've done anyway.

Why would they punish him and not me?

I rush forward again but Charmaine grabs me, pulling me back. 'Addy, stop. We'll figure this out. Let him go.'

'Are you serious? I can't, Charmaine, I can't.'

Isaac looks at me sadly.

'As you are a winner of the trials, the Prime Minister thinks it would be too unseemly to execute you on television,' the security official at the front says. 'We're to enact your punishment now.'

He lifts his gun and shoots Isaac square in the chest. The boom of the shot causing momentary deafness.

A scream erupts from my chest as the room moves in slow motion. Just like Celeste. Just like with my parents. Isaac crashes to the ground and the security officials leave the flat. Backing out slowly. Shutting the door behind them, mocking me with politeness.

The room speeds up again and I draw in a breath. Charmaine lets me go and I fall to the ground next to Isaac, pressing my hands on his chest as blood pools around him, trying to stop the bleeding. But I know it's futile.

Tears rush out of my eyes and Isaac grabs my hands. He's cold already. 'Addy,' he says. 'Let me go.' But I can't. I won't. 'I love you.'

His face is so white, any colour he had drained altogether. He goes completely still.

'No! Isaac, no,' I shout. 'Don't do this to me. Don't leave me.'

A sob escapes my chest. I can barely see him through the water falling from my eyes. My chest cleaves open at the sudden loss, and I can't move. I just stare at his cold, dead body.

I don't know how long I sit there for before Charmaine sits next to me.

'We should check his pulse,' I say, numbness spreading through my entire body.

'There's so much blood, Addy. I don't think we need to,' Charmaine says softly. She crouches down next to me, putting her hand on my arm. 'We have to go.'

I look at her, anger filling my entire being. 'I can't just leave him.'

She clenches her jaw. 'You have to. We have to go. Pack a bag, get any money you have and do it quickly.'

She drags me up from the floor and I stumble against her.

This isn't real. It can't be.

Thirty minutes ago, we were sat around the table laughing and joking. We haven't even cleared it yet; our paper crowns discarded around us, leftovers on the table.

I don't move. If I close my eyes and count to ten, everything will go back to the way it was. But when I open them, it's still the same. All the life has been sucked from the room, taking any part of mine away.

Charmaine pushes me into my bedroom, I don't know how, and makes me sit on the end of my bed. She grabs a backpack, filling it with clothes, toiletries, the essentials. She shoves a pair of hiking boots on my feet, tying them quickly.

'Where's your money?' she asks.

I've gone numb, the tears have stopped. I can't feel a thing. I just want to lay here and fall apart. Let the world forget I ever existed.

My cheek stings and I look up at Charmaine standing above me. She slapped me. I lift a hand to my face, barely feeling it.

'Come on, Addy. The money. Where is it?'

I look into the bathroom. 'In the bath, behind the siding,' I say, but my voice doesn't sound right. It isn't my own.

'Great,' Charmaine says, running out of the room for a screwdriver.

She works at the siding quickly, shoving the thousands of pounds I've saved into my backpack. I'd known something like this would happen where we'd have to run. I just assumed Isaac would be with me.

Charmaine raises her eyebrows at me and closes the zip on my bag.

I shrug. 'Needed it for a rainy day.'

She gives me a tight smile and makes me stand again. She puts my coat around me and shoves each of my arms inside, zipping it up for me like I'm a child. We exit the room, and she leaves me alone for a minute while she gets her own things. My eyes zone in on the body in the room. The blood that has stilled. The chest that will never rise again. The eyes that will never shine with love and humour. The only man who has ever really seen me. Gone, taken from the world in such a cruel way, so quickly. Will anyone even be told?

Charmaine runs out. 'I'll text James on the way. He'll have someone collect the bo—Isaac. We'll bury him when we can, I promise.' She pulls me toward the door. 'Your phone, where is it?'

I look at the sofa where I left it. And she nods. 'Good. Leave it. We'll get you one of ours.'

And we leave the flat. I take one look back at the last place I would ever be whole again. Leaving my heart behind, as I turn into who I must become.

My name is Adelaide Taylor, and they have broken me.

CHAPTER
TWENTY-SEVEN

I collapse onto a beanbag. The room is silent. At least I think it is.
If anyone is talking, I don't hear them.

Just trust me, okay? I love you, he'd said. *'I'm ready to go.'*

What did that mean? Did he know it was coming? He lays in front
of me, but not, he's not here, he's back at the flat. A team has been
sent, led by Celie to see to him. I didn't realise she'd come back. But it
doesn't matter. Nothing matters anymore.

Blood coats my hands, my dress, my legs. Hard now after the
walk—stumble—over here. When was that? How long have I been
here?

Celie crouches in front of me, putting a warm mug in my hand.

'I'm sorry,' she says. Her voice quiet, barely there.

I'm barely here. His love was the only thing I had left to believe
in. He was all I had left. And now he's gone. Another thing taken

from me, and I just want to disappear. Not in the way we'd planned. I want the ground to open up and let me crawl inside so I can be surrounded with nothing but my insurmountable grief. I feel like I can't breathe. What's the point when I don't have someone to share air with anymore? He was the better of the two of us, the stronger of the two. He could have done so much more.

I don't think I'll ever know peace again.

'You should drink,' Celie says, pushing the mug up to my mouth.

I take a sip. Hot chocolate and something else. Whiskey, I think, with the way it burns all the way down my chest. The sound comes roaring back to me, so loud I drop the mug.

It crashes to the floor, stopping the noise, and I look up. Everyone is staring at me.

'I'm sorry,' I whisper.

Sympathetic looks are thrown my way. But not by James's second-hand man, Brendan. He stands against the wall, arms crossed, watching me. What for, I don't know. I try to stand, but my knees buckle, and I almost fall. Celie catches me.

'Hey,' she says softly. 'What do you need?'

I look down at myself, at my blood-stained skin and she nods. 'Everyone get back to business. Tomorrow is a long day, and we need to get organised.'

Brendan scowls at her. 'You're not in charge just because James isn't here. I am.'

She leads me away, rolling her eyes. 'Then *do* something instead of standing in the back scowling like a creeper.'

His scowl deepens. 'Why are you even back?'

She clenches her jaw. 'None of your business. I'm taking Addy upstairs, tell everyone to stay away.'

She pulls me up the stairs, towards the old staff rooms where there are some showers.

She pulls my coat off, then my shoes. 'I don't—' I don't what? I need the blood off me, I need his death off me. 'Where's Charmaine?'

'Looking for James.'

'Why?'

She stands, looking me in the eye. 'He'll know more about what happened, about why it happened.'

I nod, like it makes sense. Like any of this makes sense. But nothing will ever make sense again. He—*Isaac*—is gone. Taken.

A cold chill takes over me as I step out of my clothes and under the hot water. It does nothing to stop the chill. Nothing to stop the thoughts running through my head. He did nothing to deserve a death like that. But I'll make sure it won't go unavenged.

When I'm clean, when no trace of Isaac is left on my body, I step out of the shower into the towel.

'What do we do now?' I ask, my voice steady and clear.

Celie frowns. 'What do you mean?'

'They need to pay for this. What's happening tomorrow? I'm ready to be part of it.'

Celie shakes her head. 'That's not for me to decide.'

'Then take me to James.' A look of worry crosses her face and I roll my eyes. 'I'm fine now.'

'He *just* died.'

My chest contracts but I ignore the need to collapse. 'And if I don't focus on my anger, I don't think I'll survive.'

She seems to think this over but finally nods. 'Yeah, okay, I get it. Get dressed.'

Some green combat trousers and a black t-shirt has been laid out for me with underwear and I dress in them. A brush sits next to them, and I untangle my hair, plaiting it back. I look at myself in the mirror. At the still red eyes, the hollow void inside me.

I'm ready for war.

The war council begins, and James explains what will happen tomorrow. The Prime Minister will be making a speech in front of Number 10 and then will be in meetings in the Houses of Parliament all day. We're to make all of this as inconvenient as possible, with protests all around the area.

He pulls me to the side.

'You don't have to take part in any of this,' he says, his hand on my arm.

I flinch away from his touch, so casually caring that I almost believe it. 'It's about time I stopped being a baby and did something. I *need* to do something.'

He stares at me, his eyes glowing with something. Some idea he has. A light bulb switches in his head.

'The Prime Minister ordered his death.'

I still. 'Why just him?'

He shrugs. 'I don't know, maybe he thinks you're more valuable.'

'But I'm no one.'

His eyes tighten, like he doesn't quite believe me. 'It doesn't matter. Isaac is dead and you're not.' I flinch at his words, but he goes on. 'Do you want to make him pay?'

I glare at him. 'Of course I do,' I snap.

He smirks. 'Then I have the perfect plan for you.'

He leads me downstairs, down into the basement where the gun range is. He goes to the wall where they're stored and takes one out.

'Do you know what this is?' I shake my head. 'It's a bolt-action sniper rifle.'

I raise my eyebrows. 'How do you have something like that?'

He shrugs. 'Some of my people were in the army, they have access to all kinds of weapons.'

A shiver rolls through me at the thought of James having something so violent.

'Okay, so what about it then?'

'Practice with it.'

He shows me how to put it together, how to load it, then how to aim and take a shot without hurting myself. I hit the target what feels like thousands of times before he stops me. Some of the anger has seeped out of me. The gun feels good in my hands, it makes me feel like I can do something that gives me purpose, like I'm the one in control.

'So now what?' I ask.

'Tomorrow, while the rest of us are protesting, you're going to kill the Prime Minister.'

CHAPTER TWENTY-EIGHT

I turn away from the target, and stare at James, my mouth gaping open.

Isaac's death must be making me delusional. That's the only possibility. There's no way James just said we're going to kill the Prime Minister. And not only that, that *I'll* be the one doing it.

I look at the gun in my hands, the feeling of power slips away.

'You can't be serious,' I say, hoping I'm imagining what he'd said.

'Deadly,' he says. Was that a pun? If it is, he doesn't laugh. 'The Prime Minister and his government are responsible for all our pain. Isaac. Your parents. They're why we're doing all this.'

I close my eyes. I can't believe I'm having this conversation. I dig my nails into my palms, the pain is harsh but it's real. This conversation is real. We're talking about actually killing the Prime Minister.

'But why do we have to kill him? Isn't our goal to overthrow them?' I ask, trying to find any other solution.

James smiles grimly. 'I wish that were a possibility, but this is the only way.'

I think back to my conversation with Celie, back at my house, and frown. 'Hold on. If he dies, whoever his child is becomes Prime Minister.'

James clenches his jaw, and he won't look me in the eye. 'That's not going to happen.'

'Why?' My brows furrow, I can't think of any way out of it. 'That's the law.'

He just shakes his head and lets out a frustrated sigh, like he's talking to a child. 'You're just going to have to trust me,' he says.

I feel like I'm going to break at any second, like the darkness is going to come and whisk me away and I'll be lost forever. I need something to focus on, I guess this is it.

'Fine, whatever,' I say. 'But why does it have to be me?'

'You told me you wanted to make them pay. That you wanted to avenge Isaac.'

I nod. 'Sure, but I could do anything. There must be someone else who can do this.'

He shakes his head and sighs. He takes the gun from my hands and turns his back to me as he walks across the space to put it back into the cupboard against the wall.

'There is no one else,' he says without turning back to me. 'Everyone already has assigned jobs for tomorrow. Except for you.'

So I'm not special. I'm not just being chosen for this because he thinks I'd be the best at it. And why would he? I'm barely trained in guns. And if I get caught, I don't know any of his secrets. Well, not enough. I'm basically no one.

That's not entirely true though. I'm a winner of the trials. Everyone knows my face. Everyone knows what the government have supposedly given me. But they don't know what they've taken away.

'It would be making a statement,' I say quietly. I pick at my nails while I try to come to terms with this. The small action keeping me focused.

James turns back to me. 'What was that?'

I stand up straight, almost determined. 'It has to be me. It would make a statement. I'm not their puppet, they can parade me around and pretend they've given me so much. I'm their trial winner after all. Positioned to join them once I've gained my degree.' I take a deep breath. 'If I kill the Prime Minister, it'll show everyone else they can rebel. It'll show everyone they don't have to live like this. We can really take control.'

Excitement fills me. I can really save us all.

A grin takes over James's face. 'Now you're getting it.'

Determined, I cross my arms and smile back. Not a happy smile, I don't think I'll ever do that again. No, this is filled with anger. They'll know my wrath before the end the day tomorrow. They'll know what happens when they thoroughly break someone.

My gaze locks with James's. 'Tell me what I need to do,' I say.

James rubs his hands together. 'So, here's the plan...'

CHAPTER TWENTY-NINE

I stand on the roof, the steps where my target is to appear in clear view. I can't believe how lax the security is, how easy it was for me to get up here. It's like they want this to happen. The air smells like snow, but it can wait. The crowd beneath me swells, the sound drowning out my thoughts. A show is what they came for, and a show is what they'll get. Hungry vultures waiting for their pickings, for their gossip. Any minute now, my target will appear.

My target. As if the Prime Minister is just any other old soul. James was right though. Taking him down will bring them all down.

This is the only way to avenge Isaac. And he's right. I finally see it now. See how this has been the way all along. With the Prime Minister gone, maybe we could make some real change.

The crowd below erupts as the target steps out. The Prime Minister. This is it then. My final showdown.

I take my gun out, putting each piece together. Would Isaac want this? Would he want me to turn into a killer just to avenge his death? I shake myself. It doesn't matter what he would want, he's gone now.

I put a bullet in the gun and take aim. But I step away for a moment. If I do this, am I any better than they are?

'No, you're not, Addy,' a voice says behind me. Janesh. I didn't realise I'd said that out loud. Muttering under my breath.

I turn around, too fast, knocking my balance and almost falling. 'What are you doing here?'

He looks at me, eyes wide. 'What am *I* doing here? Addy, what are *you* doing here?'

'I need to do this,' I say turning back around.

'You don't. You're not a killer.'

I give him a cold smile. 'Maybe I am. Maybe you never really knew me.'

He puts a hand on my arm, dragging me around to face him again. 'Isaac wouldn't want this.'

I glare at him. 'Don't say his name.'

'Don't do this.'

I shake my head. 'I have to.'

'Why? Because *James* told you to? He's been waiting for this moment since you joined. Waiting for something to tip you over the edge so he could use you like this. You *have* to see that.'

'He couldn't have predicted this would happen. Besides, if I don't do this now, when will it end?'

'If you do this, what do you think will happen? The government won't dissolve. Someone just as bad as him will take his place.'

Wasn't I worried about this last night? And James made me see the truth, that I'll help bring around a revolution. I say as much to Janesh.

He scoffs. 'If you believe that, you really are just like him.' I flinch. 'He's lying to you. It's fucking *James*. How can you of all people not see that? Hasn't he always manipulated you? Even before this?'

I can feel myself breaking apart again. I don't know what to say. He's right. He's telling me exactly what Isaac would. James is a liar. Everything he said last night was just a manipulation, he let me come to the conclusion by myself, but he would have no doubt convinced me some other way. I'm drowning in so much grief, I would have probably believed anything.

Tears threaten to spill as I say, 'It's over for me now anyway, I don't think I can go on anymore.' My voice cracks.

'If you do this, then you're exactly what James wants you to be. His mirror.' I flinch, his words cutting me. I never want to be like James. 'Do you want to know what he said that made me come here?'

I straighten. 'What?'

'I heard him telling Brendan his plan had gone completely right. That *he* was responsible for Isaac's death. That he pushed him too much. He thinks that after this, you'll finally be his.'

I suck in a breath. 'No, you're wrong.'

His face falls. 'You know I'm not, Addy. This is exactly who he is. Who he's been all along.'

I shake my head. If he killed Isaac, and then I kill the Prime Minister—no. I can't do it. I drop the gun, letting it clatter to the roof.

'We need to go,' he says.

241

I nod, letting him grab my arm and pull me down the stairs. The realisation of what I was letting James turn me into takes over, punching me in the gut. He was moulding me to be his equal.

But I don't want that.

It wasn't the government that broke me this time, it was *James.* It's always fucking James.

My face hardens. I want to be better than him, I have to be. He'll never be free as long as he's plotting against the government like this. I need freedom. If I have nothing else, then that's what I need.

The radio attached to my belt buzzes to life. 'What's going on, Addy? It should have been done by now,' James says.

I unclip it to answer. 'I'm not your pawn, James. If you want him dead, do it yourself.'

'What about Isaac? Don't you care that he is dead because of that man?'

I stiffen. 'Shut the fuck up, James, and keep his name out of your mouth. I'm leaving.'

'Don't you dare, Addy. I'll kill—' I turn the radio off before he can finish his threat.

Sure, he could kill me now. But at least I'd be with Isaac then. A sob breaks from my chest. I didn't even realise I had started crying.

We leave the back of the building to find Charmaine waiting for us, a crowd forming behind her as they push to try to see the Prime Minister's speech.

'What's going on, Addy? What were you about to do?'

I shake my head. 'It doesn't matter. I didn't do it.'

Her shoulders sag in relief. 'Good. You both need to run. Now. Some shit is about to go down.'

242

I frown. 'Isn't everyone just protesting.'

She gives me a look like she feels sorry for me. 'I told you it was too dangerous for you to be here, and you still believed it was just protests?'

'Then what is it?'

'It doesn't matter. Both of you need to go.' She hands me a piece of paper with an address on it. 'Meet Ivy and Celie at this flat on Craven Street. Your bag is there.'

She pushes me, trying to get me to walk. 'But what about you?'

'I need to see this through.'

'What? No, you don't. Come with me. We need to run. I can't lose you, too.'

She gives me a small smile, but it doesn't reach her eyes. 'I'll be fine, Addy. I promise. You won't lose me. You need to go to Dorset. Find Amy.'

My cousin? 'Amy? What does she have to do with any of this?'

'You'll know when you get there. I'll come to you as soon as I can.'

I nod, crushing her in a hug. 'Be safe.'

Janesh and I run. The speech has finished, so we have to push through crowds leaving the edge of Downing Street, and it takes longer than I'd like. We need to get away from this area. Annoyed faces glare at us, but they move just the same as we shove through.

We keep running through the crowds as cars leave Downing Street, heading all the way around the corner to the Houses of Parliament.

We're almost at Craven Street when the bomb goes off.

Chapter Thirty

The floor disappears as I'm thrown into the air. Rubble from the ground and buildings crash down before I do. I throw my arms up to shield my face from the harsh concrete.

My skin scrapes off as I land. The air is knocked from my lungs. I lay there trying to catch my breath, but it won't come. I turn onto my back, but I'm met with grey debris and smoke masking the sky, taking the day away as it coats me and makes me cough.

My ears ring, I can't hear anything as I push myself up. I pull my coat over my mouth and nose and try to take a steady breath. The smoke still clogs my throat, and more coughs wrack my chest. I turn and see Janesh sprawled on his back with his eyes shut. He has a small cut on his forehead, but otherwise looks fine.

I shake him carefully and he wakes.

'What happened?' he mouths.

I shake my head and point to my ears; I can't hear him. I don't know what happened. My eyes widen and I stand quickly. Charmaine. *Charmaine*. She's back there.

I try to run but pain spreads through my ankle and I stumble. Tears spring from my eyes against the smoke. She can't have been part of that. I won't believe it.

Sirens, long and loud, almost like the ones from the blitz sound. I can hear them. My ears start to clear. I pull Janesh up.

'We need to get to the flat. Charmaine said she'd meet us. She's fine,' I tell him but I'm really trying to convince myself.

He shakes his head, almost like he doesn't believe it, but I refuse to believe anything else.

We run along the street as people start coming out of their homes, out of their businesses. Down an alley and up some stairs. We bang on the door, begging to be let in.

Celie opens the door. She stands there for a moment, checking us over, for what I don't know. But quickly, she's crushing us into a hug.

'I thought you'd be too late,' she says, her voice cracking.

'Water,' I say, my voice barely a whisper.

She nods and pulls two bottles out of a bag.

I down mine, some of it leaking onto my face. I walk into the flat. Celie shuts the door behind us. There's not much in this room. Just a pale grey sofa, probably from IKEA, and a TV. There's a door across from me but it's closed.

'What *was* that?' I ask, sitting on the sofa.

Celie sits with me. 'James's real plan. I think he knew you'd fail and thank God you did. He blew up the Houses of Parliament. He wanted to be the new Guy Fawkes,' she says with an eye roll.

'Fucking prick,' I say, finally catching my breath.

Her eyes harden. 'At least we know now. I don't know who helped him though. None of us were kept in the loop except Charmaine.'

I nod, my chest feels like it could implode. 'Will she be okay?'

Celie avoids my eyes. 'I don't know. She didn't plant the bomb though, she would have gotten there too late,' she says. 'I guess we'll find out soon.'

Screams sound from outside, and I stand up to look out of the window. I hide most of my body behind a curtain, and peer through. The flat is cold and has a musty smell like the heating hasn't been on for a while. I don't know if this is a safe house, or if someone was living here.

The crowd I so desperately tried to get through less than twenty minutes ago streams along the street below us. Their clothes are dark, covered in debris. Someone is being carried between two people, as if they're trying to walk to a hospital. I don't know where the closest one is. Or if the unconscious person will survive. There are cuts and blood on so many of them walking and running. How many people are back at the bomb site, dead with nobody carrying them away? Is Charmaine lying dead among them? There's nobody other than me who can identify her now. A shiver goes through me—I refuse to believe she's dead. I just hope she got away.

From behind me, I hear the TV turn on. I sit back on the sofa.

I nod. 'Charmaine says we need to find my cousin in Dorset.'

'Where?' Janesh asks, finally able to get a breath.

'I'm not sure. Poole, maybe? I don't even know where she was living last.'

Celie shushes us as a news presenter comes onto the television.

'*It is with a heavy heart,*' he begins. '*That I must tell you all that Prime Minister John Anderson is dead. Multiple bombs were set off as he arrived at the Houses of Parliament this morning. There are no survivors. As is the law created when the coalition came into power, he will be succeeded by his son.*'

He appears on the screen. His dark hair combed and gelled to the side. He's wearing a tailored suit. He's stepped into a new world, and it's like the past thirty minutes hasn't happened. But they have. Otherwise, he wouldn't be stood there.

'Shit,' Celie says. 'Shit. He's his fucking *son!* That's why he never told me more.'

My mouth drops.

James is the new Prime Minister.

CHAPTER THIRTY

My family lived in Poole. Or at least near there. I know that's where we need to start, but as long as James knows we're alive, we need to lay low. He knows my past; he knows something I don't; he'll expect us to go there. So we go to a small, abandoned village in Ringwood, Burley.

Nobody really lived here anyway, the houses dotted around the area were too expensive for most. There's a flat above one of the shops that I loved as a kid. The white walls look stark against the black window frames. The sign painted above the door has been so battered by the weather it's almost gone. But I'll always know the name.

We go in through the front door of the shop, the bell ringing to let nobody know we're here. They left behind all the stock when they ran. Dreamcatchers dangle from the ceiling, collecting dreams from the dead. They lay in the grass behind the building with makeshift headstones.

The shelves remain the same, just left in disarray. In the middle of the shop is a cabinet full of crystals. I take a piece of yellow jasper. I once read it was good for anxiety. I don't know if it'll help much now. We walk to the back of the shop, where a round table sits covered in dust and abandoned tarot cards.

We go upstairs into the flat, into what will be our new home for who knows how long.

We can't stay here forever. Just for now.

There's electricity in the flat still. Like most houses, it was never cut off just in case the government wanted to use them again.

We all sit around the small, bare living room, plugging the aerial into the old TV and turn on the news. It's cold in here. I feel like I'll never get rid of the freeze that took over my bones days ago when James was announced as the new Prime Minister.

We saw on the front of a newspaper that James is addressing the nation for the first time today.

The news starts, they rounded up some rebels close to the explosion, the ones who were protesting. They weren't in the inner circle and didn't know James's real plan. He used us all. But for what reason, I don't know.

The news anchor introduces James. Standing in front of Chequers. He's had a haircut and it's gelled back. He wears a black suit and tie, like he's mourning the father he killed.

He looks into the camera.

'*My father was a great man,*' he starts, and I can't help the laugh that escapes me. He had us all fooled. '*He brought this country together after years of insanity. I plan to continue with that legacy. Some of the rebels that belong to the so-called Children of the Realm are still at large.*'

Four pictures appear on the screen: Ivy, Janesh, Celie, and me.

I feel sick. Well, that's it for us now. How are we going to find Amy if everyone is looking for us? Everyone already knew our faces, but this will just cement the image to their minds.

At least Isaac is dead, so he won't be hunted, I think to myself. Pain flashes through my chest, my heart breaking all over again. I wish he was here; I wish we'd ran when we wanted to. Part of me wishes neither of us ever entered the trials. I was just over a year away from turning twenty-five. I was so close to being on my own without being monitored. I don't know what kind of life I would have had, but it would have been something.

But I would have never met Isaac. And that's something I'll never regret. I just wish we had more time. If only we had run, I wouldn't be here alone without him. And he wouldn't be dead somewhere. I don't even know where he is.

James continues, *'Three of these rebels deceived us in the worst way. They won the first trials, they were given a monthly stipend, a home, and an education. And this is how they repay us? This will not be tolerated. If anyone knows anything about their location, you must report this immediately.'* We're really on the run then. *'The trials will be going ahead next week. One hundred criminals have been chosen for them. A list will now be shown. Thank you for accepting me, and goodnight.'*

The list shows mostly names I don't know. Then Brendan's name appears. He was James's second in command, I thought of all people he would have been safe. I guess none of us should have trusted James.

A few more names appear, none that I know. Some of the rebels were killed in the explosion. We don't know who. We hope some made it out. I don't see Yu-Jun's name, but she also isn't on the list of wanted. That's just the four of us. I can't help but wonder if she was part of the bombing, or if she stayed back to monitor the situation from Covent Garden. Maybe James did trust someone after all.

I cling to the hope that the one I care most about made it out of the explosion before she was caught. I have to hope she'll find us, even if she won't know where to go.

And then her name appears on the screen. The final participant of the next trials:

Charmaine Grant.

To be continued....

Reviews

Enjoyed Children of the Realm?

Then please leave a review on Goodreads and Amazon!

Every review you leave warms my heart. They're incredibly important for indie authors, such as myself. And every time you write a review, you help me reach more people!

Thank you, from Lauren :)

ACKnOWLeDGmenTS

I fell in love with dystopia a long time ago – ten years ago to be exact. But I've loved escaping to new worlds since I was a child. In fact, I used to pretend there were many doors in my bedroom that would take my to a new land. I always wanted to become a slayer. Then a mortician (Tru Calling anyone). Then a vampire. Always a vampire. And then came Katniss, and Tris, and Kitty (Pawn). And finally came Kyla, from the Slated trilogy by Teri Terry, who is a huge inspiration to me.

All these female characters became part of who I am, and I can only hope that Adelaide inspires my readers in the same way.

This book wouldn't be possible without my amazing editor and proof reader, Rebecca Holmes. Thank you for the gift you have given me with this book. And sorry for all the complaining haha.

And my cover and interior designer, Connie May. I really don't know how you put up with my endless paragraphs of panic but thank you so much for all the hard work you've put into these books.

My beta readers, thank you all for reading the book and helping me with *that* decision. I can't promise book three won't be worse.

My mum who will have still not finished reading the beta copy by the time this comes out, thank you for all your support.

This book took a little longer to write than the first. I wrote Trials of the Realm during one of the lockdowns, but I had a job by the time I was writing this one. So I'm so glad I've been able to have the time needed to get this done.

And finally, thank you to all my readers. Whether you be Kindle Unlimited, paperback or ebook readers. You're all helping me become a better author. I'm so thankful for those of you I found on tiktok who love my book as much as I do.

Thank you for reading!

ABOUT AUTHOR

Lauren Stabler loves to read and explore new worlds. Her active imagination has afforded her many opportunities to create worlds in her head. But when she couldn't find books that matched the stories, she dreamt up for people her age, she decided it was the perfect opportunity to write her own.

She holds a BA and an MA in Creative Writing from Sheffield Hallam University. When she's not writing, she can be found reading, playing the Sims, her absolute favourite game, or spending time with her long-haired ginger cat, Maisie. She lives at home with her mum and stepdad in Sheffield.

Printed in Great Britain
by Amazon

20374108R00150